The Druid Legacy

Book 2

Dungeon

Contents

Chapter 1: Scouting

The first indication that the grelkin and Listranni had arrived were several columns of black smoke from the edge of town. Commander Marsh stood next to me on Swansea's western wall. I am sure the commander had a perfect view of the town, looking over the crenellations. That's the big blocks the archers hide behind on the top of a castle wall. Since I was about a foot shorter than him, I had to look through the merlon, those were the gaps designed to shoot arrows at attackers.

The commander turned to me. "Wess, do you think you could go take a look? I am curious if any of them have deserted since you took out all of their leaders. See if they look well formed-up or if they are running around loose. Also, see if you can spot any giants. Same question about them, I need to know if they are on their own or if someone is commanding them."

I smiled back at the commander and said, "No problem sir, anything else while I am out? Some fruit from the market, perhaps?"

The commander scowled down at me. During the last week, I had gotten to spend a lot of time with him and it was my intention to make him laugh at something. He seemed to only have scowl muscles in his face.

I shrugged and climbed onto the merlon. That is what they call the space between the crenellations on a battlement. I had spent a lot of time up here, so I got to ask my archer friend, Steve, a million questions about walls and castles. It was a pretty uneventful week, but now I knew everything about castle design.

I leapt out from the wall as far as I could. The walls were about thirty feet high above the town, but the ground on this side sloped downward away from the castle, so the height was greater. Steve said this made it harder to roll rams and catapults toward the walls. Plus, he said, tired invaders are easier to kill.

I was so excited to be doing something and flying was one of my favorite things. I couldn't resist scaring the archers gathered next to the wall. They had been standing up here in shifts for a week wearing ring mail and helmets and I was sure they were all bored out of their minds, just like me.

Falling with my arms outstretched and the buildings rushing up at me, and shifting my shape into an eagle at the last possible second gave me plenty of speed. My open wings caught the air easily, and a screech of joy escaped my throat as my dive turned into flight. Climbing away from the walls, heading toward the fires, I gained some height as I flew so I could get a better view and remain out of the range of anyone with a bow below. I was sure the grelkin would have enjoyed a delightful leg of eagle.

In this form, I had much better vision than my human eyes allowed. I could see for miles. Two giants were busy trying to catch and eat cows at a nearby farm. The farmer had let them out on the range, and the cows had scattered at the site of the giants. It was pretty funny watching them try to catch the cows. They were about thirty-five feet tall , and they were running stooped over with their hands out wide trying to herd the cows toward each other. When the cows got close to either giant, they broke left or right. The giants looked confused and not sure which way to go. They came together with no cows between them and immediately started arguing about who was "stupider." I decided that I didn't need to worry about the cows.

I banked to the left and soared over the market. I was surprised to see a lone giant lying in the square. He must have walked here last night. He was sleeping directly in the center of the circular market. Around him, every cart was overturned. I knew the commander wanted me to stick to scouting, but I felt like this was too big of an opportunity to waste. Giants were hard to kill and this one was making it too easy.

I thought about forming a rock spike under his head, but I thought that might just wake him up angry. I didn't know if I could form that spike fast enough to break through his thick skull. When I asked rock elements to help, they didn't move as fast as water and I had not practiced using them as a weapon. I hadn't even thought of the idea until now.

I circled back around and considered my options; I didn't like any of them. This creature was humongous and looked like he could crush me with his finger. I felt my resolve waning and was sure that I was about to talk myself out of this. I pictured this thing scooping up my friends and popping them in his mouth. It made me angry to think about all the townsfolk this giant had chased from their homes. They were up in the castle sleeping in tents or the mess halls because of this invading army. Here was my chance to do something about it and I was going to fly back to the castle a scared little boy?

The circles I was flying in had gotten tighter as I got angrier. I decided to act before I lost my resolve. I tucked my wings, diving toward the giant's neck. At the last instant I flared them back out, landing and transforming right next to him. As I did, I willed my axe, Azurain, to my hands. It appeared there changing its blade shape to be longer and thinner even as I was chopping down on the giant's throat. It sliced easily into the giant's massive neck as I cleaved down with all my strength.

Blood sprayed me in the face, and I staggered backwards raising my arms to try and shield myself. The giant let out a burbling scream and flailed his hand toward his neck. I dove to my right, barely avoiding the giant's hand as he clutched at his neck. I tucked and rolled to a stand. The giant turned away from me trying to rise, still screaming in rage.

He pivoted quickly from his knees, looking for the source of his rude awakening. Blood pumped steadily from between his fingers and his eye locked on me. I froze in place, not sure what to do next. The giant bellowed and dove toward me, swinging his huge fist downward to smash me into the ground.

I transformed again, armoring myself in rock as the giant's hand smashed into my head. The force was so powerful it flattened me. My rock form held, but it hurt a lot. The giant stood and picked me up by my legs holding me upside down in his fist. He pulled me up to his face to look at me, still clutching at the wound in his neck. I was upside down, but I thought he looked a little wobbly as he stood.

He furrowed his massive brows at my rock form, and then started slamming me into the ground. The impact sent rock chips flying from me, and my mind reeled with each hit. The combination of hanging upside down and being slammed rapidly into the ground was making it impossible to heal myself. I worried that I was going to lose concentration and drop the rock form, so I focused all my efforts on maintaining it. I was sure that if my armor failed, I would be dead with one smash.

The giant finally muttered, "Too dizzy..." and fell on his face.

I pried his fingers open and stepped away from him. I released the rock form and started healing my wounds. Scanning myself with my gift, I found that I was bruised everywhere. I felt like someone had clubbed me all over. I borrowed a little regenerative energy from the earth and pulled it into me, I felt better immediately.

The giant was dead or dying, so I felt like I shouldn't stay here any longer. I was sure his yells had attracted attention. I leapt up and shifted my shape to the eagle form and tried to flap my wings.

As I transformed, I heard a grunt close behind me. Confusion and pain battered my conscious thought as a spear pierced my shoulder from behind. I pitched forward and fell on my face, pain blooming up through my arm. I looked down to see the spear point protruding from my shoulder, blood pouring from the wound. Only then did I realize that I had dropped my concentration and snapped back to my human form.

The sound of a sword pulled from its sheath saved me; I scrabbled left as the blade struck the cobblestone where my head had been. I moved Azurain to my left hand and clutched the shaft of the spear with my right as I stood. Pain shot straight to the top of my head as I stumbled away from my attacker. I turned and continued to move, still trying to distance myself from harm. My attacker was a short, fat grelkin who was smiling wickedly as it stalked toward me, waving its sword left to right.

My right arm had no strength now, and I was a total spaz with my left. I didn't think I could hit a barn if I threw my axe with my left hand. I continued to backpedal, searching for any way to defend myself. My vision blurred, and my knees shook.

My mouth went dry when I spied movement from my left and more grelkin came pouring into the market square. I wasn't going to stand there and count them all, but they were coming in from every alley and opening. They swarmed over the dead giant and whooped in joy at my plight.

I turned from them, back to the grelkin smiling triumphantly in front of me and said, "Well, today is a nice day to die, I guess."

The grelkin lunged forward, pulling his arm back to jab with the sword. I tried to lift my axe to block it with a sideways swipe, but my arm felt like lead and I wasn't moving fast enough. Even my fuzzy brain could see there was no way I was going to be able to block his strike. The grelkin grabbed my shirt with his left arm and stepped close to drive his sword up through my gut. It was so close to me that I could smell rotten meat from his mouth. The sad thought crossed my mind that I was going to leave this world while smelling grelkin breath.

I felt a rush of air on my cheek as a large spiked ball flew past me trailing a familiar rusty chain. The ball struck the surprised grelkin full in the face and it fell dead, killed instantly by the powerful strike.

The grelkin's whoops of joy turned into screams as mounted knights charged into them from a side street. Yells of, "Swansea!" echoed of the market walls. I was sure I also heard one yell, "For Wess!"

In my befuddled state all I could think was, "Hey, that's me!"

I stood there, losing blood, dazed and unable to think clearly. My half-ogre friend, Ben, came to stand near me, winding his chain up. The knights carved swaths of carnage with their long lances through the unorganized grelkin. Once Ben had recovered his spiked ball, he placed himself between me and the scrambling horde of panicked grelkin. I saw several of the monsters try to flee our way, but each time, Ben would throw his spiked ball and a grelkin would die. At eight foot tall with huge tusks, Ben probably looked scarier to the grelkin than the knights, even on horseback.

Finally, the market had cleared out and the knights began to reform their lines. Ben turned back to me and looked down at the spear point. Once again, I was impressed by his range of expression. He looked all battle-fierce while killing grelkin, but now his eyebrows shot forward and he looked seriously concerned for me.

I looked up at him, smiled and said groggily, "Hey, nice to see you."

He reached out and almost touched the spear point, asking in a deep and gentle voice, "Hurts?"

I stood there swooning and threatening to fall over. The loss of blood was affecting me; it was like trying to pick out one voice from a crowd of people all talking to me. After a moment, I nodded and said, "Yeah, it hurts a lot."

Ben nodded then bent to scoop me up. He held me out away from his body to try and make the ride smooth for me and began striding back toward the castle. I was barely able to hold my head up, and the motion of Ben's stride made me feel like I would pass out.

I felt like talking would help me avoid slipping into darkness. My tongue was thick, and my voice sounded slurred as I asked, "So, Ben are there other half-ogres? Did the Kurzak make more of you?"

Ben looked down and raised an eyebrow at me, "Yes."

I smiled and rolled my head around on his massive forearm, "That's good, Ben. Maybe one day you could meet a lady half-ogre."

Ben just frowned down at me and continued walking.

Rolling my head back and forth felt weird. I felt my head moving, but my vision moved slower than my head. It felt like I had sludge between my ears.

I prattled on, "Do you think we will see Hannah Bear again? I wonder if she will remember me. Where did she go after you left the cave with her?"

Ben smiled, shaking his head and looking down at me like I was an idiot. Finally, he said, "Elf."

Ben normally spoke in only one word answers. Once he said two words together, but he usually chose words that make sense. I never felt like Ben was stupid, I had seen evidence that he was quite clever. I decided my fuzzy head was playing tricks on me. Maybe I had heard him wrong. "Did you say elf? Like pointy ears elf?" I asked, my voice slurring.

Ben just nodded without looking at me.

"Huh, I don't know what elf has to do with Hannah Bear. I am so sleepy. I think I am just going to close my eyes a little."

My voice sounded far away and my eyelids felt like they weighed a ton. I wasn't feeling pain any more, just a weird slowness. I heard distant shouts around me, and I was vaguely aware that people were talking about me. I felt my movement change subtly. I thought Ben might be placing me onto a table or something.

I was almost asleep when I realized one of the voices belonged to my friend, Arish the Medicus. I felt hands on me, and through my groggy thoughts I made out counting. I thought, "That's weird, why is he counting?"

I realized too late that Arish was counting down and when he got to zero Ben yanked the spear through my body. I was surprised that I didn't feel more pain. There was a tugging sensation, then pressure on the spot as I was rolled onto my back. I tried to heal it, but I only managed a tiny flow of energy. I felt the wound close a little, but the effort pushed me over the edge and I blacked out.

I don't know how long I was out, but when I started to wake, I felt the familiar flow of healing energy from the earth that I had come to know too well. I was lying with my eyes closed, enjoying the warmth spreading through me. It wasn't me doing it, but it felt very familiar, like a hug from my mom or dad. It made me feel good and I smiled.

The healing warmth abruptly shut off, and I heard a familiar voice above me, "There are those on the council who would have let you die."

I opened my eyes to see Melikin the Arch Druid frowning down at me.

I sat up slowly and looked around the room before responding. My father and Arish were both present. My father looked concerned, and Arish looked in awe of Melikin. Arish endeavored to heal people, but had no gift with magic at all. He made up for it with hard studies and many hours of candlelight reading. I think he would have given anything to be a Druid.

"It's good to see you too, Melikin." I said.

Melikin spread his hands, "I was hoping you would have come to me for training by now, Wess. It would be a shame for the greatest potential Druid in our time to have his life cut short by a single grelkin with a rusty spear."

I frowned and looked down at my shoulder. I wasn't aware that I didn't have a shirt on and the scar from the spear was prominent. I blushed in embarrassment when I looked back up and everyone was staring at me. "Sorry, I have been kind of busy. I need to help clear the grelkin out so I can go rescue my mother, then I promise I am on my way to you for training."

Melikin grew agitated as he spoke, "These human problems are not your concern Wess. I need you to come to training now!"

My father turned toward him and interrupted him angrily, "Last I checked, that was not your call since he isn't *your* son, Melikin."

It was the first time I noticed that Melikin was considerably taller than my father. It didn't seem to bother my father as he shouted up at him, but Melikin was at least a half a head taller.

Melikin frowned down at my father and lowered his voice, "Actually, it *is* my call, Lucas."

With that, he stepped around my father and came to stand next to my bed. I felt awkward lying in bed and looking up his nose, so I swung my legs down, raising myself to a sitting position.

Melikin started again, "The Druid council called a meeting and demanded that I rein you in. The Lord Druid Felizion was most unhappy that someone with your power and potential, yet untrained and unprotected, was walking around with Azurain."

He paused, then added, "The Elven Protectorate believes you should be killed and the artifact hidden to prevent a potential catastrophe. In her words, it isn't a question of if a twelve-year-old boy makes a mistake, but when it happens, how much of the world he will destroy in the process. You represent a threat to all of the naturekin and the world if you remain untrained, Wess."

I was shaking my head even as Melikin was relaying this. My father looked like he was about to pull his greatsword. I don't think he liked the idea of someone wanting to kill me. I held up my hand to let him know I was going to speak.

"I hear what you are saying, Melikin, but you tell them that I am going to rescue my mother. I promised that I would come to training after I did that, and I will." I stood up, searching for my shirt.

My father spoke quietly, and he sounded calmer then I would have thought, "Wess, maybe you should go with Melikin now."

I looked up in surprise and asked, "How can you say that, Dad? What about Mom? You want me to leave her with Rissling?"

My father's face looked pained as he thought about how to say what he wanted to. Finally, he said, "Wess, you know that your mom wouldn't ever want you to put yourself in jeopardy to save her. I will be going after her myself with the King's support after this invasion is over. You were almost killed last week."

"Whoa... Last week? I have been out for a week?"

Arish spoke up, "You have been out for five days with an infection and severe blood loss. The spear tip was coated in some kind of feces. We almost lost you, and I am not sure that we wouldn't have if Melikin hadn't come."

18

"Feces, what is that?" I asked.

I looked around, and everyone was smiling. Melikin was chuckling a little.

Arish finally answered me, "It is a common practice amongst the cruder races, or so I have read. They coat their weapons with excrement so that if you do survive the cut, the infection eventually kills you. It is quite effective."

I looked around, still confused.

"Poop," my father said. "Excrement and feces are just fancy words for poop, Wess."

Everyone started chuckling as I looked down at my wound in horror. "He stabbed me with a poop spear? Gross!"

Arish chimed in, serious as ever, "Gross, but devilishly effective. You have to admire their creativity. They lack the ability to craft more sophisticated poisons, but they have shown a certain cleverness here."

I gave Arish a dead stare and said, "Really? Do I really have to admire their creativity? He stabbed me with his poop!"

Melikin and my father both seemed very amused by all of this. Just then the door crashed open and I saw Ben's muscled arm holding the door open for Myka. She walked in slowly, moving a little stiffly. She was smiling ear to ear and holding what looked like a new shirt for me.

I was so happy to see her walking again, but it was hard for me not to feel guilty every time I looked at her. It was my fault her spine had been injured, and I was unable to heal her without causing her tremendous pain whenever I tried. I didn't think I would ever forget the site of Myka lying in the courtyard with an arrow sticking out of her back.

She limped toward me, and I stepped forward to hug her tightly. I smelled her hair as I hugged her. She smelled like pears. Finally, she pulled back and spoke loud enough for everyone to hear, "I am glad to see you up. I would have hated to engrave 'Killed by Poopy' on your tombstone."

"BWAHAH!" Ben ducked inside and barked out a short laugh. He grinned with his tusk-filled mouth, patted me on the head, and said, "Poopy!"

The room was getting crowded, and I was becoming embarrassed by the fact that I still wasn't wearing a shirt. Myka helped me put it on. It gave everyone in the room time to quit laughing at the idea of me being killed by a poopy spear.

"How about we step outside and talk there?" I asked.

Ben shrugged and said, "Okay."

I found this funny because Ben didn't participate much in any conversation. He mainly spoke with his facial expressions or his spiked ball. The question had actually been directed at Melikin, who seemed happy to go along with Ben's agreement.

Arish stayed inside, but the rest of us filed outside. It was dusk, but there were still soldiers drilling in the courtyard. A squad leader was shouting out orders, forming the men up in various defensive formations. I watched the formation switch from a square with their shields facing forward to a circle with their spears pointing out and their shields in a ring. It looked fine to me, but the squad leader screamed about how they were never getting to eat tonight. It made me realize that I was positively starving.

Behind me, I heard Melikin ask, "Excuse me young lady, but can I ask why you are limping?"

I turned to see Myka looking at me, unsure what to say. I answered for her, "I did it. It was an accident. I was showing off for the commander, and I made a whirlwind deflect a bunch of arrows, and one went through her spine." I looked down, unable to meet Melikin's gaze before continuing, "I tried to heal her, but I wasn't good enough, and at first she couldn't move her legs at all. She is in pain every day because of me."

My dad put his hand on my shoulder and pulled me in for a sideways hug. Everyone was silent, and I still couldn't look up. Finally, Melikin spoke to Myka, "May I try?"

I looked up feeling hopeful. Myka nodded, and Melikin made a spinning motion with his finger indicating she should turn around. He looked at me and said, "Wess, come here and put your hand on mine."

Melikin placed his hand on the small of Myka's back, and I felt him take hold of the earth powers. I stepped forward and stood next to him, placing my hand on the back of his. "Close your eyes if it helps you to see what I am doing with the flows," he whispered.

I did, and I could see he was already sending a tiny probing flow into Myka. I was surprised by how little energy he drew and used. His probe was no wider than a thin thread, where mine was the size of my wrist. He wound it gently through Myka's spine and down her right leg.

After a moment, he spoke again, "I can see where she was injured Wess, and honestly, you did pretty well in repairing the damage. A little earth energy to block the pain and some water element here will do the trick, I think. The hard part is to hold the two energies separately in the right place."

I watched in awe as he maintained the probe and brought forth a needle thin water flow and a second earth flow. When I pulled energy it was always a large and wiggly thing that struggled against my will, but this was precise and under his total control. He delicately slipped the water element inside Myka's spine and placed the earth element right above it. I watched as he healed her gently from the inside while holding the two flows in total control. He was precise and delicate where I was kind of blunt and forceful. His skill maintaining multiple flows from different elements while flowing healing energy showed me that I had an immense amount to learn.

I heard Myka's sharp intake of breath and my eyes popped open, worried that Melikin was hurting her. Melikin shut his flows off quickly as she leapt away from us and did a little twirl. She let out a laugh of pure joy and said, "You did it! Thank you, thank you, thank you!"

I swallowed the lump in my throat, torn between feeling joy that Myka was healed and the disappointment that I wasn't the hero. It was small of me, but I had to admit that I was feeling a pretty strong resentment toward Melikin and pretty hefty dissatisfaction with myself for feeling that way. I looked up at Melikin and forced myself to say, "Thank you, Melikin. That was very kind of you."

Melikin raised his eyebrows at me and appeared ready to say something.

Before he could respond, there was a scream from the top of the castle wall. My head whipped around as the wall exploded from the impact of a huge boulder. It was dark at the top of the wall, but chunks of stone and a body rained down into the torch-lit courtyard below.

My father was the first to react, sprinting toward the wall before the last stone fell. Ben followed quickly behind him. With his long legs I was sure he would beat my dad to the wall. I moved to follow, but Melikin clutched my shoulder.

I looked up at him as he spoke, "This is not your fight, Wess, come with me."

I shook my head, resolute in my decision. "These are my friends, I won't leave them when they need me. I am not coming to training until I rescue my mother. What is the point of all this power if I can't help my friends?"

Melikin looked sad, "That is what I need to show you, there is a much greater point to all this power."

I think he could tell that I wasn't going to budge. I just stood there and crossed my arms, stubbornly refusing to speak. He stared at me for a moment, then his shoulders slumped and his hand dropped from my arm.

He spoke softly, "Ten days, Wess, then the council will come for you. That is all I can grant you."

I started to argue, but he leapt away from me and transformed into a large barn owl. As he was flying away, he spoke in my head, the way he had when he taught me to shift, *"Ten days Wess, don't waste them."*

I ran for the wall. As I got closer, I could see that it was still standing, but was badly damaged. The breach extended from the top of the wall to form a V extending down to the middle. Lots of people were running for the steps up to the top, but I ran for the body I had seen hit the ground. I was hoping I could heal the unfortunate man who had plummeted to the courtyard. I had to slow down because of all the loose stone, but I finally found him.

He was lying at an odd angle, covered in stone dust, and not moving at all. I reached out with my gift, but I could tell right away that he was dead. The spark of life had flown from him long before I had arrived. I bent down to roll him to a less awkward position and saw the eyes of my friend, Steve, staring lifelessly back at me.

I was not expecting to see my friend lying there dead. I felt like I had just been talking to him about how bored we were.

Suddenly, there was another thunderous impact at the wall and more stone showered down around me. I clenched my teeth, rage starting to build inside me. The giants that did this to Steve were still out there, in the dark, hurling boulders, my Father or Ben could be the next victim.

I leapt away from Steve and envisioned myself as a giant barn owl. I thought the vision of an owl would be very helpful at night. I had not tried this form before, but I was a fast learner and I was confident I could do it. I shifted quickly and pulled with my wings toward the top of the ruined wall. I was so angry that I barely noticed how well I could see in the dark as I crested the fortification and flew out over the town.

It didn't take me long to see three giants standing in the market square. One was throwing boulders toward the castle and the other two were bringing him rocks and other large objects to hurl. I climbed higher and summoned my natural powers. My rage moved me to act without even considering my options. I pulled in the clouds above the giants and formed them into one massive storm. I forced them tighter and tighter and made sure that they didn't rumble.

I waited until both of the giants were near the hurler. I cast out as wide as I could and felt a massive volume of energy at my command. I thrust it sharply into the cloud and yanked downward with my will. All three giants looked up as the largest lightning bolt I had ever seen crashed down into the hurler.

The flash blinded me and broke my concentration. I transformed back to my human self instantly and plummeted toward the town below. As I tumbled out of control, my heart leapt into my throat and I tried to transform again. I had shifted into an eagle plenty of times, but trying it while spinning in a free fall was much harder.

I finally shifted my shape into the familiar form, but I was upside down. I twisted and flapped hard. I spun and realized I was about to crash into a building. I made the snap decision that I couldn't pull up in time. I released my form and with the strength of my will, forced my rock armor into place as I slammed into the building.

I hit the wall at an angle, still traveling forward from my flight and smashed through it. I struck two or three more barriers before I finally stopped. I rolled to standing and released the rock armor. The armor had done its job, and I was extremely thankful that Melikin had shown it to me. I looked around and willed Azurain to my hand. It felt good to hold my axe, but I didn't see anyone in the building to use it on. I was in a warehouse of some sort, surrounded by pallets of goods stacked in sections.

Looking up revealed the hole I had made on entry. It went through the roof, that was the floor of loft above me, and the outside wall. There was movement out of the corner of my eye and through the window I saw lots of grelkin moving around outside. I crept over and peered out. The window gave me a clear view down an alley toward the market. Carts lined the left and right, but most of them had been destroyed or emptied by the invaders. The grelkin were running toward the market shouting in their strange tongue.

I decided that I needed a closer look and being on the ground was making me feel uncomfortable. I leapt away from the window and changed into the owl form again. The night vision proved useful as I flew up and out of the hole I had created.

Exiting the building, I banked left, continued to climb, and flew over the alley toward the market. I was shocked at what I saw; the lightning bolt had been remarkably effective against the giants. The giant who was struck directly had exploded from the impact. Blood, bone, and charred flesh coated everything in the market. The other two giants were lying dead next to the crater, their bodies blackened and twisted. They had died with looks of extreme pain frozen onto their faces.

I looked down at the grizzly scene and couldn't help but be impressed with myself. Grelkin were pouring into the market and arguing about what they were seeing. I landed on the roof of a tall three story inn that overlooked the market to observe them. I smelled the strong scent of cooked meat and weirdly, it made my mouth water. I still hadn't eaten, and I couldn't help thinking about a nice juicy steak. It was seriously gross thinking of food while I was gazing down at the charred giants, but I couldn't help it. I was starving.

I thought about sharing this story with my friend Steve and it renewed my anger. The good people of Swansea didn't ask for any of this, and I wasn't going to let myself feel guilty for killing the enemy while I defended the town.

My conviction renewed, I reached out with my power and found the thunder cloud was still largely intact. I poured more energy into it and released my bird form, standing to reveal myself to the grelkin below.

I knew that not all grelkin spoke English, but I was hoping some of them would. I yelled down at them, "I killed them! I have killed four giants, and I will kill you all! Leave here and never return!"

With that, I made it rain and start to thunder. The grelkin just looked confused and began arguing. One of them appeared to be translating what I said, and they were looking from him to me.

I let him finish, then I called down my first lightning strike into the crowd. This time, I was smart enough to close my eyes as it lit the air. Even though my eyelids, everything turned white in an instant. My hair stood on end, and the bolt exploded below me. Grelkin flew, screaming, burning, and dying. The bolt arced between them, and a moment later the thunderclap followed. The windows around the market shook with the blast and the grelkin that lived shrieked in fear.

They panicked, crashing into each other in a frenzied attempt to escape. I pulled again and again, each time lightning striking wherever I willed it. I focused my efforts on larger groups of grelkin, but I was killing so many of them that it was quickly becoming hard to find targets. They fled from the market square and I leapt from the roof, changing into an owl to give chase. I was going to ensure they got the message. It was time to end this.

I flew in widening circles and anytime I saw a group trying to form up, I struck at them and they scattered. I kept at them for a while, and I found myself near the edge of town. It became harder and harder to find targets, and I felt fatigued. Finally, I turned back toward the castle and opened my wings to glide. I released the cloud and my hold on the energy, realizing only then that I was well and truly exhausted.

As I flew over the wall, I was glad to see that they had taken Steve's body away. I didn't want to see it again. My rage had completely left me now and I just felt sad. I was sad about Steve, but also about all the creatures I had to kill tonight. I didn't like having to do it.

In the courtyard, there were several squads forming up and the commander was giving orders to his leaders.

I made a wobbly landing next to the commander and dropped my form. I wasn't trying to be dramatic, but I was so tired I thought I might drop the form in flight if I stayed in the air any longer.

Commander Marsh swiveled his gaze toward me as I shifted. With his short red hair and face that only had one expression, I couldn't help but feel like he was always angry with me. "Wess, report!" he barked.

I gave him a groggy smile and said, "I'm fine sir, thank you for asking."

He stared at me, waiting for me to get to something he cared about.

I sighed, "I killed three giants and hundreds of grelkin with lightning strikes. I believe the siege is broken sir. They are fleeing."

Even as I was finishing, the squads started muttering and whispering to each other. Some in the back couldn't hear everything, and I heard what I had said whispered down the ranks.

Commander Marsh glanced at the men, then at the squad leaders. He did not look happy at the lack of discipline.

The squad leaders acted without instruction and turned to bellow at the men in their respective squads. I was guessing that having a booming voice was a requirement to becoming an officer.

I stood there, shifting back and forth on my heels, wondering if I should sneak away or just sit down and hope someone brought me food. I felt like it would be embarrassing to fall flat on my face in front of all these men, but it was a real possibility.

The commander stepped toward me and in a lowered voice said, "There is only one thing better than a dead giant, Wess, and that is three dead giants. Nice work, soldier."

I looked up at him and smiled, "Soldier, huh? Does that mean I get a helmet?"

For the first time since I had met Commander Marsh, he smiled. "I don't think we have one that would fit that tiny head of yours, but maybe we could have the blacksmith work on something for you."

"Oh, a custom helmet? Could I get one with horns? That would be sweet!" I said hopefully.

He gave a chuckle and patted me on the shoulder. I staggered and almost fell over. He said, "Why don't you get some sleep, Wess? I will have the steward bring some food up."

I raised an eyebrow at him, shocked by his consideration.

"Thank you, sir. That would be great."

It was a day of firsts: this was the first time he smiled at me and the first time I wasn't smart to him.

He turned back to his leaders, and I could hear him issuing orders to get scouts into the town. I stumbled off toward my room, feeling strangely content and looking forward to the meal that would be coming. I hoped the steward was quick.

I staggered past refugees and occasionally one would say hello to me. Some of them knew my name, and I gave them a tired wave as I stumbled past.

Finally, I arrived at my door. I pushed it open and fell onto my bed face first. A wave of exhaustion hit me, and I closed my eyes. I didn't want to fall asleep, and I didn't think my stomach would let me, but I laid there with my eyes closed and listened for the steward.

The smoothest, most velvety voice I had ever heard spoke from across the room, "You are one of the highest priority targets for assassins from Kurzak and you don't even look around the room before entering?"

Opening my eyes made me think I was dreaming. Sitting at my eating table next to the door was a tall man with the head of a tiger. He was wearing a pitch black cloak with the hood pulled up, black leather pants and no shirt. He was lean but solidly muscular. Light white fur covered his chest and stomach fading to orange and black stripes toward his back. On his belt, he wore a dirk and a short sword. His right hand rested comfortably on the table, his left draped casually over the back of the chair.

As I sat up and rubbed my eyes, he spoke again, "I am pleased to meet you, Wess. My name is Sevest."

"How did you get in here?" I asked.

"The door." He answered.

"No, I mean how did you get in here past the guards and all the townsfolk? I mean you almost can't go down the hall without stepping on one, so how does a tiger-man walk past all that?"

Sevest turned his paw up and asked, "Is that the pressing question, really? Usually, the first question is *what are you*?"

I pulled myself backwards and leaned against the cold stone wall. If I was dreaming, I believe I would have made myself think quicker. I was about to ask what he was when there was a single knock on the door. I looked at Sevest who gave me a little grin but didn't move otherwise. Without taking my eyes from his, I said, "Come in."

The overly handsome steward Myka had fawned over at our picnic came in with a tray of food. Sevest moved his hand slightly toward the steward, but otherwise held perfectly still.

"Your dinner, sir, where should I place it?" Mr. Good Looking asked.

I looked back to Sevest, but he was staring at the steward.

"Umm, on the table will be fine."

"Very good, sir." He set the tray down right in front of Sevest and pulled the lid off. I saw steam rising from the plate and my mouth started watering.

"Baby carrots, shepherd's pie, and bone bread, sir. Will there be anything else?"

I looked from Sevest to the steward, "Um...maybe another cup for my friend?" I gestured toward Sevest as I asked.

The steward seemed confused. He looked at Sevest then back to me. "Are you expecting someone else, sir? I can have a second meal prepared if you like?"

I was pretty sure the steward couldn't see the cat-man sitting right in front of him. I wondered if that meant I was nuts. If I was going nuts, would I be sane enough to think I was going nuts, or would I assume everyone else was nuts?

"Sir?"

"Oh, sorry, no never mind, this will be fine. Thank you."

"Yes sir, have a good night." With that, he backed out and closed the door.

Sevest looked at me and gestured to the food. "You should eat, you look as if you might start drooling."

I didn't need to be told twice. I moved quickly to the food and grabbed the bread, tearing off a large chunk. I dipped it into the gravy and started shoving it into my mouth. I don't think I have ever been so hungry. In between my bites I managed to ask a question of my feline visitor, "Sevest, how come the steward didn't see you?"

Sevest drummed his right hand on the table, and I noticed he wore a ring on each finger.

"It is good for him that he didn't," Sevest said. "I do not wish to be seen by anyone in this castle, except for you. I have come to make you a proposal, Wess. Would you care to hear it?"

I stuffed more food in my mouth and thought about the fact that he didn't answer my question. I shrugged, "Why not? I mean you traveled all the way from...?"

Sevest grinned and said, "I am from a minor house in Kurzak. Rissling created me many years ago, but now I serve no one but myself."

He paused to let his words sink in and I looked up from my food, studying him anew. "That must be an interesting story, I can't imagine that was Rissling's idea."

Sevest tilted his head a little, "That is a perceptive observation, Wess. The food must be working because that is the first one worthy of your reputation."

"I have a reputation?" I said with my mouth full of bread.

Sevest smiled; it was unnerving. "Oh yes, you are quite the topic of conversation in Kurzak. I believed that much of what I had heard was exaggerated, until I saw you kill three giants with a single lightning bolt."

I gulped down my water and tried not to smile. I couldn't help but feel strangely excited that people in a foreign land were all talking about me.

Sevest continued, "The boy who has managed to make enemies of two houses in Kurzak is all the nobility are discussing these days. I would have given much to see you cut Goering's head off myself. I never liked Lord Algrier or his little pet. You did us all a great service by dispatching the beast. He has been sulking in his estate since his sudden return. I dare say that no major house has ever suffered such an inglorious defeat. The other houses have secretly commissioned bards to write songs to celebrate your achievement."

I stopped chewing and stared at Sevest. "That can't be good."

He answered casually, "It has been very good for the minstrels, but certainly won't be for you or Swansea. Lord Algrier is the master of a major house and has substantial resources, which he has now dedicated to killing you. Rissling is a gnat compared to Lord Algrier, but now they work with a common purpose."

I slumped and muttered, "Great." I shoved some carrots around with my last bite of bread. I sighed and asked, "All right, what is your proposal?"

I looked up at him, and he tilted his head slightly, "I would like to offer a trade of services. Rissling is prepared for you and has built elaborate defenses designed to stop you. He has placed your mother in a dungeon and cast spells that will prevent your magic from working, even with Azurain in your hands."

I was surprised that he knew about Azurain, but I didn't want to show it. He was enjoying this way too much, and it was bothering me. He smugly raised an eyebrow at me, and I leaned back gesturing for him to continue impatiently.

"You will try to rescue your mother within the ten days that the druid council has allowed, of which you have nine left, and Rissling will kill you. He will then gain control of Azurain and advance his position as a house. This will not be good for me. I propose to change our fates, Wess. Are you interested?"

I replied, "I am interested to know how you know about the ten days."

"I am sure that you are, but that is not what I asked you," he growled back at me.

"You won't answer a straight question, but you expect me to?" I asked.

"Please, Wess, do not act as a petulant child. It is unbecoming of a dragon slayer or giant killer such as yourself. Do you wish to hear my proposal or not?"

I didn't know what petulant meant, but I was pretty sure it wasn't nice. I did like the sound of Wess the Dragon Slayer. Maybe I could get a badge or something. I pictured a dragon's head with a solid red line through it on a shield as my coat of arms. I realized I was staring off at the wall behind Sevest. I was still extremely tired. I looked back at him and nodded, defeated in this minor war of wit.

"My proposal is straightforward, Wess. I will rescue your mother from Rissling, and in exchange, you will perform a task for me. I will not be overly challenged to remove your mother, as I am perfectly suited to the task. You will not be overly challenged to retrieve the item I seek, as you are perfectly suited to the task I have for you. Do you wish to hear the details?"

I was leaning forward now, excited by what he had said. I nodded.

He continued, "I seek an item that has been hidden by the naturekin for many centuries. It is in a location that one must have an affinity to the natural elements to be allowed entrance. These elements should be friendly to you, but alas I have not been gifted as you have. I will provide you with a map to this item and you will go and fetch it for me. In exchange, I will risk my life and certainly gain the wrath of two houses by rescuing your mother."

He paused and I took that as my signal to ask a question. "What is this item that you want me to retrieve?"

He considered his response for a moment, then answered, "It is a torque, an artifact lost since the great wars. It was used against the naturekin almost three hundred years ago, and they guard it to ensure it will never be used against them again."

"And how do I know you won't use it against them?" I asked suspiciously.

He leaned back in his chair, "I have no quarrel with the naturekin. I seek to improve my standing and gain power over my fellow Kurzak houses. Achieving more power would allow me to work against the much larger houses. That is something that would benefit you immensely. Ever heard the expression, *the enemy of my enemy is my friend?*"

He stopped then, and we both stared at each other. I wasn't being dramatic. I was still exhausted, and my brain was working slowly. "I also have to free Myka's father, Mr. Millen. Will you rescue them both?"

He dipped his head, "It should be an uncomplicated matter. I would likely just purchase him from his owner. This is a fair condition. I accept your terms. Do we have an agreement?"

I felt like I had been painted into a corner, but I didn't see a better option. Finally, I nodded and said, "Show me the map."

Chapter 6: Journey

A storm was coming, moving in from the south, which was the direction I was going to be heading according to the map Sevest had given me. I looked out from the undamaged southern wall at the town below. As the shadows of night began retreating from the rising sun, I could see patrols of light horsemen clearing the town in organized patterns. They posted green flags on buildings to show they were clear. I assumed Commander Marsh wanted to ensure all the grelkin were gone before allowing the townsfolk to return to their homes and work.

I wanted to leave early this morning, but for some reason I was having trouble talking myself into it. My heart was heavy, and I thought about the note I left for my dad, Myka and Ben. It said simply that I had to go do something that would help free mom, and I would be back within about a week. I said that I needed to move quickly so I couldn't take them. I didn't want to give any hints as to where I was going, so I didn't mention the naturekin connection requirement of the mission or Sevest. That was a condition of my agreement with Sevest; I was never to talk about him. I knew my friends would try to talk me out of going, my dad may even forbid it, but I was feeling guilty for sneaking out without talking to them.

Sevest had given me the ring I had taken from Uncle Jourg and told me how it worked. I questioned how he got it, but he just asked me in an exasperated tone if I would ask

42

how a bird flies. I got the very clear impression that Sevest didn't like being questioned. He told me that he had set the location of the ring to his estate, where I should return when I had acquired the torque. Lastly, he instructed me not to touch the torque directly, but to wrap a bag around my hand and pick it up that way. He said that it would be very bad for my health if I did touch it.

I had everything I needed to get going. I just didn't want to take the leap; I was stalling. A big part of me wanted to go hug Myka and my dad before I left. I was nervous about the journey, but I felt like everything Sevest had laid out for me made perfect sense. I guess that is what was bothering me; I felt like this agreement was too perfect.

Well, I wasn't getting it done standing on this wall. I sighed and fell forward, diving off the wall and shifting into my favorite form, the giant eagle. My heart lifted at the feeling, the pure joy of it helped me feel good about what I was doing. I didn't think I would ever grow tired of it; I loved the feel of flying.

I soared over the town, barely having to flap my wings. The wind from the oncoming storm made it easy to glide. Before I knew it, I was flying over the farms outlying Swansea and rapidly closing on the line of thunderstorms. The clouds looked low and angry, and I wasn't sure what I should do. The line was long left to right, and so tall that I didn't know if I could make it over them. As I got closer to them, they looked even higher than I first thought.

Lightning danced along them and thunder rumbled, giving me serious concerns about flying through them.

I decided to fly lower, and as I did I felt the temperature drop when I reached the storm. I thought about trying to control the weather, but if controlling a storm this large would have consequences. I pictured causing a drought in Faermont by changing this one storm, it was something I thought I should ask Melikin about when I went for training. I flew into a wall of rain and the wind started buffeting me hard. I struggled to fly, but was tiring quickly from the effort.

I looked below to see a thick forest filled with old growth trees. There was no clear path through the trees that I could see. The rain started pounding hard, and the wind shoved me down. I scanned the trees and found an opening, diving downward to avoid the storm. As soon as I broke through the thick canopy, the wind and rain lessened considerably. I dodged a few branches and landed, releasing my form to shift back to my human shape.

I pulled my hood up, but I was already soaked through. I started to shiver as I looked around, considering my options. The storm made this old forest dark, and it was so thick that I was sure I couldn't run through as a horse. I walked forward through the brush and spoke aloud to myself, frustrated, "Well, this is an excellent start to my heroic journey!"

I heard a sweet female voice behind me, "Heroes don't kill trees!"

I turned just in time to see the old oak tree I had just walked past whack me in the face with a branch. My feet flew up, and I landed hard on my back. The root of the tree shot up and wrapped around my chest. My eyes bulged as the root threatened to pull me underground.

I quickly pulled some energy and tried to make the tree stop. The tree ignored me. Instead of releasing me, more roots shot out from the ground and wrapped around my legs.

"These are my trees, Wess, they will not obey you!"

I looked to the tree and saw Larissa the wood nymph step from the oak, glowering down at me with her hands on her hips. The storm raged and the wind roared, blowing her light green hair into her face. She angrily pushed it back and narrowed her almond shaped eyes at me. I couldn't help but notice that she was wearing a short skirt made of leaves and vines. She turned into the wind and put her hands back on her hips and screamed at me, "How could you do it, Wess? How could you kill all those trees?"

I screamed back, trying to be heard over the wind, "I'm sorry, Larissa, it was an accident! I was trying to heal a girl's finger and I pulled too much energy. I didn't know what I was doing then! I still don't, but I'm trying, Larissa."

"I knew those trees, Wess! You treated them no better than the grelkin did. They chopped them down to build their stupid fort!"

I thought she was crying, but I couldn't be sure as the rain was soaking her. I squinted up through the drops stinging my face and asked, "What can I do to make it right, Larissa? I promise I didn't mean to hurt them!"

She crossed her arms and swiveled behind the tree, shielding herself from the wind and rain. She stood there with her arms crossed staring at me. She seemed to be considering what to do with me as I was pelted by the storm. Finally, she turned back to me and said, "You need to think about what you have done. I think I will leave you here for a few years."

"A few years?" My voice raised to a shriek and cracked a little. I hoped she couldn't hear it over the wind. I cleared my throat and tried again, "I am a human, Larissa. I will be dead in a few days if you leave me like this! I need to rescue my mother. If I don't do it in ten days, the Druid council will come kill me!"

Larissa stuck her tongue out at me. I thought this was kind of immature for someone that was 73, but for all I knew 73 was a child for wood nymphs.

I tried again, "Larissa, can you please let me up? I need to go get a torque from the naturekin."

As soon as I said torque, her head whipped toward me, her eyes going wide. Lightning struck and thunder rumbled. She was shouting something at me, but I couldn't make it out. As the thunder trailed off, I heard her finish. "...elves, so I might as well let you go!" she said.

I watched with my gift as she turned and walked into the tree. I studied how she did it and now that I had seen it again, I thought I might be able to do it. As soon as she walked into the tree, she moved her essence out of it, and I watched her travel away, connected to the energy of the forest. As soon as she was gone I asked the tree to release me, and it complied immediately. The branch lifted back up and the roots uncoiled from my chest.

I stood up and wiped my face to clear the rain. I am not sure why I bothered; I was so wet that water was flowing from my head and cloak. I turned and stepped into the tree as I had seen Larissa do. She had pulled me into a tree once before, but doing it myself was interesting. I felt connected to the essence of the forest. I wasn't just in the tree, but I was now a part of all the trees in a way I hadn't been before.

I felt Larissa step out from a tree far from where I was now. Near her I could feel a strong natural power. I hadn't felt anything like this before. I pictured the map Sevest had given me, and I felt like it was in the right direction, so I decided to follow Larissa. I took a single step and envisioned myself walking from the tree that Larissa had exited. As I pulled myself from the distant tree, I noticed the sun was out, and it wasn't raining here at all. In front of me was the largest tree I had ever seen. It was probably twice as large as the giant I had killed.

The area was clear around the tree with a thick layer of moss coating the ground. Flowers grew in random patches, and I felt at peace. Larissa was walking toward the tree, and I could see now that she was heading for an opening at the base of the roots.

I hurried to catch up and called out to her, but she didn't look back or slow. She calmly walked under the tree and disappeared into the shade of the roots. I followed her in and found there was a room of sorts under the tree. Light filtered in and I could see Larissa standing next to a ring of mushrooms. She looked up at me as I walked in and spoke, "The Elven Protectorate will likely kill you on the spot, Wess. She will not be happy to see you in Laun Lauchneakin uninvited."

"The Elven Protectorate is a girl?" I asked stupidly. I regretted it before it was out of my mouth, but even more as Larissa put her hands on her hips looking angry at me again.

"Sorry, I am an idiot. Could you invite me in?" I asked.

She responded angrily, "Why would I do *that*?"

I looked down at my feet trying to think of something I could say to get Larissa to like me again. "I don't know, Larissa. I am trying to do the right thing, but it seems like every time I do, someone else gets mad at me. I don't want to make the elves mad too."

I looked up at her, and she considered my words for a moment before answering, "Inviting you in will only keep her from killing you on the spot. If you try and take the torque, she will likely kill you anyway."

I shrugged, "Well, that's better than dying as soon as I arrive, I suppose."

She looked at me and tilted her head then asked, "If I do this, do you agree that you owe me a favor?"

"I agree, I owe you one anyway for killing all those trees."

"Don't answer this lightly, Wess. A promise to a Sidhe is binding for life. You will not be able to refuse me when I ask it."

While she spoke, she walked toward me and took my hands, leading me into the ring. She looked into my eyes and asked slowly, "Wesslayn Grace, do you promise to owe me the favor of my choosing in exchange for an invitation to Laun Lauchneakin?"

It was hard to breathe with her staring at me so intensely. She was uncommonly pretty and I was struggling to concentrate. I nodded dumbly and said, "I promise."

I felt a jolt through her hands and her power shot through me passing quickly into the ground. I raised my eyebrows, and she spoke, "You are bound to your word, Wess, you will be struck dead if you refuse when I ask you. I invite you to Laun Lauchneakin."

A mist began to rise around the ring, it was so thick that I couldn't even see the sides of the tree. In a short moment, the mist covered everything outside of the ring. It parted after a few seconds, and I could see the night sky clearly above me. It started sinking toward the ground and Larissa dropped my hands, turning away from me. She walked into the mist and I wasn't sure if I should follow or not. I clutched Azurain and took a step toward the mist.

From the direction that Larissa entered the mist, I heard the distinct ring of two swords being drawn. I froze and called out, "Larissa?"

There was no answer from the wall of whiteness. I stood there holding my breath and listening. Finally, I could make out a form standing just inside the mist, which was now thinning. I was sure it wasn't Larissa as I saw two large curved blades held casually in front of the figure.

I tried again, "Umm hello, my name is Wess."

She stepped from the mist into the ring. I was surprised to see she was about my height. She had raven black hair pulled back with a leather band and a high pony tail exposing her pointed ears. She had lavender eyes and was wearing tight leather armor and boots to her knees. She was eyeing me with a hard look, and I blushed because she caught me staring at her with wide eyes.

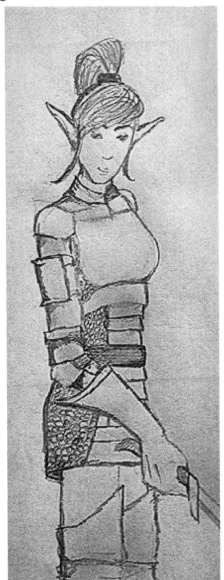

In a smooth motion, she sheathed her weapons and spoke harshly, "Larissa invited you, so I have to let you in. My human name is Samantha, I am the Elven Protectorate. If you offend the Queen, I will be the one killing you."

"Well then, I hope she isn't offended easily!"

Chapter 7: Laun Lauchneakin

The mist fully subsided, and I looked at my surroundings. Behind me was a black wall that stretched left and right as far as I could see. It was shiny and looked like it was made of some kind of opaque glass. I thought I could see shapes moving on the other side, but I wasn't sure. Around me were mushrooms of various sizes and shapes; some were twice my height. There was no grass. Instead, every inch of ground was covered in a spongy moss. I shifted my weight back and forth on the balls of my feet, enjoying how it felt.

I was thinking about taking my boots off so I could feel it with my toes when Samantha interrupted my thoughts, "What are you doing here, Wess?"

I looked up from the moss. I didn't want to answer that question yet, so I tried a tactic that I had just been used on me by Sevest. I answered her question with one of my own, "You know my name?"

She nodded, "I serve as an honorary member of the Druid council and a liaison from the elves. I am the one that tried to convince them that we should kill you now and hide the artifact."

I swallowed and nodded, "I see. Yes, I recall Melikin mentioning you. I am sure you will like me once you get to know me better." I gave her my best smile, but she appeared unimpressed.

"We shall see. Come."

She turned and started walking off down the mushrooms. I was smiling to myself about distracting her from her question when I heard the distinct ker-chunk of a catapult firing. I looked in the direction I heard it and saw a body flying through the air.

"Whoa, what is that?" I exclaimed.

I scrambled to catch up, and she answered casually, "Those are the flingers."

I started jumping in the air to try and see where the body was going, but as I watched it arced below the mushrooms and I couldn't see where it landed.

Samantha glanced back at me disdainfully, "We have to fling the dead over the walls or else they will come back on this side."

She said this like I was a moron because I didn't know this already. So, of course, I responded as sarcastically as possible, "Well duh, obviously you are catapulting your dead over your glass walls. I mean that part was obvious, for sure."

She rounded on me and jabbed her finger into my chest, "Are you mocking me?"

I put my hands up in surrender and stepped back a little, "Take it easy, lady! Did I insult your sister or something? Why do you hate me so much?"

She stepped forward, rage in her eyes, looking ready to cut me in half. She jammed her finger in my chest again and said, "*Your* kind are all the same! You are the reason we live like this! You are the reason we have to fling our dead over the walls! You are the reason we are assaulted by them! You care nothing for the sacrifice we made to save your race. If I had my way, I would kill you on the spot, so don't test me!"

I was too confused to match her anger. I just stared at her for a moment then finally asked, "Umm, I have no idea what you are talking about."

She let out a growl of frustration, spinning away from me, muttering something about humans being dumber than mushrooms.

I followed behind her, wishing Larissa was here. She was mad at me, but at least I knew why. I decided that silence was my best option. I was sure that anything I could say would just make Samantha angrier with me.

We wound our way through the mushrooms in silence, and I noticed several weird things about this place. The first was that the stars looked different than back home. I wasn't good enough with the stars to know what was different, but they just didn't look familiar to me. The next thing I noticed was that there was not a single loose rock anywhere. Lastly, there seemed to be only two plant types here, mushrooms and moss. If I was alone, I would have dug under the moss, I was very curious what I would find under it. I had lived in a forest most of my life and this place felt unnatural, more like I was in a giant bowl that someone put moss and mushrooms in to make the animals feel more comfortable. The longer I spent in this place the more sure I was that this wasn't anywhere on earth.

We continued on in silence for another ten minutes or so before we came upon a town. On first impression, I thought there were thousands of houses carved from even larger mushrooms than the ones we had been walking through, but when I looked closer I was sure that they were not carved, but grown into the shape of houses.

There were signs of life everywhere: clothes hanging to dry, trays of food laid out on outside tables, and musical instruments leaning against a wall. There was evidence everywhere that people lived here, but there were no elves in sight. It was the middle of the night, but none of the mushrooms had any doors and I couldn't even see anyone inside the homes as we walked past.

My curiosity got the better of me and I whispered to Samantha, "Where is everyone?"

I don't know why I whispered, but I felt like I an intruder. Samantha glanced at me like she had forgotten I was there. Her annoyance was still obvious as she answered, "At the flingers. We don't just casually shoot our dead over the walls without ceremony."

We crested a slight rise and Samantha stopped and pointed. There were thousands of elves lined around the center of the town. From here, I could see they formed a circle around this cleared area. In the middle of the large clearing was a massive catapult, made of that same black glass as the walls. Two robed elves were slowly carrying a body wrapped in linen toward the strange machine. The elves around them were humming and rocking back and forth rhythmically. Standing by the catapult was another elf wearing an intricately embroidered white robe. We were too far from him for me to hear, but it looked like he was reading from a large book. Behind him was a wide palace grown from a single gigantic mushroom.

Samantha seemed to be waiting, so I looked around with my gift. There was natural energy everywhere around me, but I felt something weird emanating from the palace. I felt like someone was pulling at me from inside. It made my palms itch and I gripped Azurain harder.

I released my gift and glanced over at Samantha. She had her head bowed now, so I looked back toward the catapult. The man in the white robe pulled the lever, releasing the mighty arm and launching the corpse. The body arced through the air and the two carriers were left holding the linen shroud. From this vantage point, I could easily see the wall as the body disappeared behind it.

Samantha raised her head, and all the elves stood together. The man raised his hands to the crowd, and they started to disperse, many of them walking back toward us. Samantha spoke again, this time her voice softer. She whispered, "They were brother and sister."

She saw my confused look and pointed at the wall, "The two we flung today. They committed suicide together. I knew them and their family for over four hundred years."

I was looking at the wall as she spoke, but now I looked back to her and said, "I am sorry Samantha, obviously, I came at a bad time."

She shook her head slowly, "No, it is I who should apologize to you Wess. I was angry because I should have been at the ceremony, but it is my duty to greet intruders or invited guests."

"Why would they kill themselves?" I asked.

She stood there staring at the catapult for so long that I thought she wasn't going to answer me. Finally, she whispered, "This land we are forced to live in is a difficult place to thrive. It is eternal night here, and the dead never rest. Except for the Sidhe, no one can leave through the portals. It is a difficult existence and elves live a long time, but even with all that, I am furious with them. Suicide is never acceptable, but I can't help but feel partly responsible. Maybe if I found a way to get us all back home…"

"I see, where are we exactly? And why are the elves forced to live here?" I asked.

She shrugged a little, "Sometimes I forget that most humans weren't around during the Great Wars. The only ones I normally talk to are Druids, and most of them were alive then."

She collected her thoughts as elves filtered past us. I received some strange looks, but no one spoke to us. Finally, she said, "During the Great Wars, there were seven artifacts held by various races. It started with the one held by Nelzeroth, Azurain, your weapon. He was a champion for good, but the other countries and races felt like he would use it to subjugate them eventually. There was a great effort to find and recover all seven artifacts. The seven together would make someone nearly invincible. Some of them were found by men with large ambitions and the Great Wars began. No one ever held more than two, but I shudder to think if someone had. That much power corrupts everyone eventually."

She took a deep breath and looked around. "We didn't live here then, we lived in your world. It was a beautiful forest kingdom, a place the Druids now call the Sacred Glade was the center. There were many more of us then, and our nation was large and powerful. We had no interest in the Great Wars or the artifacts, but it came to us just the same. A human necromancer named Dernaz Al-Shaim decided that an undead elven army at his command would allow him to destroy the other nations and gain more of the artifacts for himself."

I interrupted her to ask, "Sorry Samantha, but I am not sure what a necromancer is."

She nodded and answered, "A wizard who uses dark magic to raise and command the dead. Every elf we lost, we faced in battle the next day. Can you imagine that, Wess? Fighting your own friends and family members the day after you stood shoulder to shoulder with them?"

I shook my head. I couldn't imagine it, but I am sure it would have been horrible.

She continued, "We elves had our own magic, but the necromancer had one of the seven. He possessed Crimsura. That particular artifact could take the form of any jewelry and Al-Shaim wore it as a large gaudy torque so that all the world could witness his power. We asked all of our neighbors for aid, but only the Druids came. Melikin and the others stood with us during the final assault."

"There were less than four hundred of us left when Al-Shaim showed himself for the first time. Up until then, he had sent wave after wave of dead warriors at us. We were barricaded inside our stronghold, killing undead in narrow corridors. The queen commanded us all back to the throne room. She said it was time to retreat to ensure our race could survive. She would deny Al-Shaim the joy of knowing that he had wiped out the elves."

"The Druids aided her in the casting of a powerful spell that pulled us all into this world. Al-Shaim broke into the throne room and realized we were escaping. He cast his own spell, somehow tethering himself to the queen and was pulled through. He could have let us go, he had swelled his ranks with thousands of my kin, but he was drunk with power and took offense that anyone would deny him anything. I remember the look of rage on his face vividly as he realized we were escaping. The Druids made one final push across the dimensions and entombed Al-Shaim here as he arrived. My mother, the queen, uses her magic to maintain the walls around us as Al-Shaim continues to call the undead."

"He is still alive?" I asked, shocked.

She nodded then, "We believe so. Many have offered theories, but my mother believes that he draws life energy directly from her. She has grown weaker every year she has been here, and she believes it is because of Al-Shaim. He was a very powerful spell caster, made even more powerful by Crimsura. I do believe he is still alive, maybe even thriving for all I know."

I swallowed, sure that I already knew the answer to the question I didn't want to ask. I pulled out the drawing of the torque that Sevest had given me, I asked quietly, "Is this Crimsura?"

Samantha gazed down at the drawing and nodded, asking, "Where did you get that?"

I rolled it up again and dropped it back into the sack. With a heavy heart, I said, "I am here for Crimsura. Looks like I have to kill Al-Shaim to get it."

Samantha yanked her sword out and slashed at my head in one smooth motion. I am sure that the only thing that saved me was Azurain enhancing my reactions. I dove and rolled, feeling the wind from her blade on my neck as it whistled past. Even as I stood and pulled my axe she came at me, both blades slashing in at me from different directions. Her face showed no anger, she wore the calm mask of someone who looked like she would be very comfortable killing me.

Chapter 8: Samantha

I tried calling my rock armor, but there was no rock in this realm at all. I wasn't counting on it as I hadn't seen or felt any rock element since I had arrived. All I could do was surrender to my reactions and count on Azurain to help me.

Samantha's blades flashed in at my midsection. I turned sideways and pivoted Azurain horizontal. I caught one blade on the top of the hatchet and the second on the bottom of the handle. I didn't have time to be impressed with myself, but the sound of metal on metal shot a thrill of excitement through me.

She shuffled forward without hesitation and thrust both blades toward my chest. I swiped across with Azurain and knocked both her blades past me, down and to my right. I spun in past her and tried to drive Azurain's handle into the back of her head.

She ducked and elbowed me in the small of my back. I grunted and dove forward as both her blades swung over my head. I came up in a smooth roll and blocked her first strike as she continued to spin.

Samantha pulled her blades apart for another strike and I drove toward her, closing the gap quickly. I slammed my elbow into her forehead, and she stumbled backward with a surprised look on her face. I was trying hard not to show one on mine, but I was pretty darned shocked. I wasn't thinking about what I would do, just reacting and moving with instinct. I was absolutely astounded that I managed to hit her. Now that I was thinking, I was sure she would cut me in half if we started fighting again.

"Samantha, I don't want to fight you!" I said while stepping back and lowering Azurain.

Her nostrils flared and her jaw clenched, "You think I will allow a human to have two of the seven? Did you not listen to the story I just told you?"

I shook my head, "It isn't for me. I'm giving it to a friend in exchange for a task he is performing for me."

Her eyes narrowed and she started gliding to her left, circling me. "You must think I am stupid, or you must be yourself. No one would give up one of the artifacts," she said.

"Well, I don't think you're stupid, so that may make me the stupid one, but I am telling you the truth. I don't want Crimsura for myself," I replied.

She stopped pacing and raised from her crouch. "I cannot not allow you to open the tomb! If Al-Shaim is still alive and you fail to kill him, he would be freed."

"That isn't for you to decide, Samantha," a man behind me called out.

Samantha looked around, and I took the opportunity to do the same. Lots of elves had stopped to watch the combat and many of them were standing behind me with their arms crossed.

The one who had just spoken took a step forward. "If he kills Al-Shaim then maybe we could finally go home! We could leave this cursed place!"

Several people in the crowed started talking excitedly. Samantha shoved her blades back in their sheaths and put her hands on her hips. "You can't be serious! You would risk everything on this boy?"

The man looked around to make sure he wasn't alone in his feelings. He seemed to get what he needed and turned back to her, nodding, "I can't speak for everyone, but I am ready to die fighting to leave this place. We are not thriving here, Samantha, and I for one am ready to fight Al-Shaim myself. If I died, at least I wouldn't be stuck here anymore. This is no life for an elf!"

She raised her eyebrow and looked around slowly. When she was sure she had everyone's attention, she said, "Yes, you wouldn't be stuck here. You would be an undead servant in Al-Shaim's army for eternity."

The man gestured toward the wall, "We will all become that soon enough. If it is a choice of living here and waiting for the flinger or going out fighting for a chance at a real life, I choose life! It is time, Samantha. We can't keep living this way."

I turned toward the crowd and spoke loud enough for all to hear, "I don't know that I can kill Al-Shaim, or if I did that it would allow you to go home."

I looked around, and I could see they were waiting for more. I added, "I promise, I will try to do both."

That seemed to satisfy the crowd and all eyes swiveled to Samantha, waiting for an answer.

Her gaze moved to each of them slowly, then finally, her shoulders slumped in defeat. "Fine, we will put it to the queen, I am confident my mother will make the right decision. Gureya, would you go ask Sherian to call an assembly?"

The woman named Gureya nodded and ran toward the palace. Samantha turned back to me and said, "Don't get your hopes up, Wess. My mother is a truly wise woman and I am sure she will not allow this to happen. Come, I will take you to the assembly hall."

She turned and started walking toward the palace. Once again I had to hurry to keep up. After catching up I mumbled, "Sorry about elbowing you in the forehead, Samantha."

She glanced over and raised an eyebrow at me.

I felt awkward and stupidly rushed to fill the silence, "I am sure you are a much better swordsman, um swordswoman? Swordsgirl? Anyway, I am sure you can best me in a fair fight, Azurain is probably the only reason I wasn't cut in half with your first swing."

She chuckled a little and shook her head like I was a stupid kid, which is what I felt like.

I stumbled on, babbling like an idiot, "I mean you probably have trained a lot with those things."

She interrupted me, "At least two hours daily for more than four hundred years."

I shrugged, "Well, the only training I have done is swinging my axe at firewood."

"And this is supposed to make me feel better, Wess?" She was smiling at me now.

My voice was high and I spoke too quickly as I responded, "Well, I am just saying that you are really good, and I am sure that you would have beaten me easily if you had an artifact."

She stopped and turned toward me, "If I say you are forgiven, will you stop talking?"

I looked at my feet and muttered, "Sorry, I'll shut up now."

A bell rang three times from the palace and I looked back to the town to see all the elves heading our way.

Samantha hurried on and I continued behind her, deciding to be silent. I felt awkward and unprepared when I talked to her. I wished Azurain would make me good at talking to girls, but apparently not even an artifact of immense power could handle that impossible task.

We entered a large archway in the front of the palace. There was no gate or portcullis, just a big gaping opening. We wound our way inside the giant mushroom, through hallways that all looked the same. We finally came to a huge hall with a stage and benches all formed from the same grey mushroom material. It was depressing me and I had only been here a short time. I could see why this place would pull all the joy from someone.

There was a pedestal in the center of the stage with a large round glass ball that had cloudy colors swirling around inside of it. Samantha led me to the front bench, and we sat directly in the middle.

I was going to ask Samantha about the big glass ball, but I didn't want to sound stupid again. I just sat there and acted like I knew what was going to happen next as the rest of the town filed in.

Samantha was sitting there patiently, but I was fidgeting. My knee was bouncing up and down and I was slapping my hands on my lap while looking around at everyone. I wasn't aware I was doing it, but when I am nervous or bored I have difficulty sitting still. My dad told me I would grow out of it someday, and I was encouraged to see that, at four hundred years old, Samantha was able to sit extremely still. My eyes landed on her and she slowly swiveled her head to me, meeting my eyes. She put her had on mine and whispered, "Relax, slow your heart."

I took a deep breath and tried to calm myself. I slowly exhaled and felt nervous energy flood from my chest. I closed my eyes and focused on breathing, slowly starting to relax.

I opened my eyes and found Samantha staring at me with a slight smile. "You will make a fine Druid someday, Wess."

I smiled back and she continued, "A Druid's greatest weapon is his mind. I have some elven magic from being Sidhe and it is instinctual to use it, but I have seen Melikin do things with his gift that required considerable concentration and focus. You will need to master your mind and body as a Druid."

I nodded, thinking of all the times that my concentration had lapsed and my powers had failed me. I remembered almost drowning when I dropped my eagle form after I crashed into a river. I wondered if there were exercises I could do to make my brain stronger. I decided these were better questions for Melikin and instead asked, "What does Sidhe magic allow you to do?"

She shrugged casually. "I am not that strong in my magic. I can activate and use the Fae gate to transfer back to Earth. I am not strong enough to create a new gate or to transfer others through. The queen was strong enough and if she was awake, I am sure she could bring us all home."

My eyebrows furrowed in confusion. "Wait, the queen isn't awake? How are we going to talk to her?"

Samantha looked very sad, "Remember when I told you Al-Shaim tethered himself to my mother to get pulled through the portal?"

I nodded.

"Well, she fell into some kind of a deep sleep. We keep her alive through communal magic. We feed her, and she in turn I think she feeds Al-Shaim. She communicates through the Vizuac Sphere, but it takes a great deal of communal magic to make it work, so we don't do it often." As she mentioned the sphere, she pointed to the swirly ball.

I nodded again and she continued, whispering now, "I haven't spoken to my mother in forty-three years."

My eyes went wide and I looked back toward the ball, the full magnitude of this existence dawning on me. I imagined a town that had so little happening in it that they didn't need the ruler to make a single decision in forty-three years.

A deep sonorous gong sounded from somewhere in the palace, and everyone quieted. The male elf from the catapult appeared, still wearing his white robe. He walked to the ball from the right side of the stage in slow measured dramatic steps. He arrived at the glass ball, took his hands from his sleeves and placed them on the sphere. When he did this, all the elves took the hands of the elf next to them. Samantha took mine, and a young elf to my right took my other hand.

I closed my eyes and looked with my gift as all the elves started humming. There was a purple haze forming and shaping amongst the crowd. It sharpened and formed a sort of grid pattern linking all the elves together. The man in the robe reached out his hands and pulled a strand of energy back to the ball. As it hit, the color in the ball swirled faster in response. The energy in the purple strand started to pulse and the colors coalesced into a shape. A face started to form in the sphere. I opened my eyes, looking with them and my gift. The clouds of color slowly parted and the shriveled, drawn face of an elderly female elf formed. The face looked unnatural, like it was being pulled inward by little threads. I heard Samantha gasp, and I glanced over to see her cover her mouth, a tear falling down her cheek.

The queen spoke without opening her eyes, her lips barely moving, I could hear her voice in my head, "My children, your queen is here still. My power wanes, but I may speak to you one final time before I join the weave."

Samantha stood and spoke, "Mother, you look so weak! I just visited your body yesterday and you looked fine!"

"Yes my child, I am sorry for my appearance, but as Al-Shaim drains me, I have put all my energy into maintaining the walls, and my spirit is failing, I'm afraid. I had hoped that he might die before I did, but as I grow weaker his pull only intensifies. When I fail, his tomb and the walls will fail as well."

"Mother, how much time do we have?" Samantha asked.

"A few days, a week at the most," the queen responded.

Samantha clenched her jaw and balled her fists. "This makes this discussion unnecessary, what we must do is obvious now. We must kill Al-Shaim before he drains you completely. This boy carries Azurain and he wants to take Crimsura. He will help me kill Al-Shaim."

I stood and cleared my throat, "Nice to meet you, Your Majesty, my name is Wesslayn Grace. Most people just call me Wess."

The queen's eyes fluttered but did not open. The face in the swirling mist shifted toward me slightly. "Wess, your arrival is timely, a week later and the walls would have fallen. My people would have been assaulted by the undead outside. Destiny seems to have its hand on you, and maybe us as well."

The image of the queen's face shimmered a little as I responded, "I must admit, Your Majesty, that I didn't know about your people when I came here, but if I can help you, I will."

The face blurred and almost disappeared. The queen spoke with some urgency, "You must not hesitate! When you open the tomb, his pull on me will become stronger, and the walls will likely fall. You must have the people prepared. The undead will come!"

Her face contorted in pain suddenly, "You do not have much time. Hurry!"

The color swirled around her and her face disappeared only to be replaced by a man's. He had a long face with a block chin and a thin goatee. His bloodshot eyes were scanning the townsfolk.

His voice boomed through the hall, "I am coming for you, elves! This tomb could not contain me and now you will be my eternal servants!"

Suddenly, his eyes swung to mine then he looked me up and down. His eyes lingered on Azurain for a time then he started laughing manically. Finally, he spoke to me, "Oh this is wonderful, I am trapped in this wretched existence because I sought to raise an army to take the other artifacts and you have brought one to me! The queen is wrong, boy! I am the one who has a destiny here! I will be unstoppable! YES! Come to me!"

He closed his eyes and suddenly the energy started pulsing red back toward the elves from the ball. I had a feeling that if that energy reached the elves it would be bad for them. I swung Azurain up through the strand reaching from the elves to the sphere and it passed right through it, severing it cleanly. There was a small womp sound from the strand, and I was thrown into the air, Samantha flying the other way. I landed hard on my butt and saw the first and second row of elves had been shoved off their benches. The ball had gone full color again, the faces gone.

I stood back up and locked eyes with Samantha. We both nodded at each other, sharing the thought that we didn't have much time to act. Samantha turned to the elves who were now picking each other up and raised her voice to be heard by all, "You must arm yourselves quickly and return to the palace. Barricade every entrance! Once Wess and I open the tomb, the walls will surely fall. We will give you two hours to prepare. Leave all your belongings, but arm and armor everyone you can!"

With that, the elves burst into action and Samantha strode toward me. She signaled that I should follow her, and she turned toward an exit that led to some stairs leading up. I hurried to follow and as I did, she spoke urgently over her shoulder, "Wess, I am going to take you to our library. There is a book there that chronicles what we know about

Al-Shaim. I am going to go say goodbye to my mother and gather a few things that might be helpful."

She was taking the steps two at a time, and I was running hard to keep up. After five switchback flights, we exited into another uniform grey room with no door. There were shelves carved into the wall and only about twenty books in a room that could have held ten thousand.

Samantha jogged to the shelf and grabbed a book. "We didn't have parchment, so we wrote on blank pages from other books. Anyone that knew anything about him wrote it in here in case we needed it one day."

She handed it to me, "I will be back soon, Wess. I hope you find something we can exploit."

With that, she ran from the room and I heard her ascending more stairs, two at a time.

I sat and opened the book. I think calling it a book was a bit generous. It was about ten pages of notes written by different hands.

I scanned through them looking for something that might prove useful. Most of it on the first page I already knew. There were notes about Al-Shaim's use of death magic to create undead. The writer was sure he could only raise humanoid creatures. He apparently had raised humans, elves, gnolls, and grelkin zombies. The book explained that gnolls were creatures that lived in the wastelands with the heads of jackals and the bodies of humans. There was a drawing of one and I hoped I never had to meet it.

In the margin someone had doodled the words, "Only death magic or other schools of study?"

Page two was all about Al-Shaim's history and had been written by Samantha after they had come here. She documented several trips back to earth through the Fae Gate to research Al-Shaim. It talked about how Samantha had discovered that Al-Shaim's mother had kicked him out when he was thirteen. She had been his first murder victim and first failed experiment. Apparently, she was some kind of nobility.

The next page had a small sketch of his family sitting together. Even in the sketch, the artist had captured Al-Shaim's disdain for his family. The boy stood apart and wore a slight sneer. I studied the picture for a while before turning the page.

Page four was notes about Al-Shaim's tomb, written and signed by Melikin. It made sense that he would have come here to inspect it. He believed that the tomb trapped Al-Shaim between dimensions during the transition. His theory was that it may have created a space where Al-Shaim could actually live and maybe even thrive. Lastly, he detailed the tether that Al-Shaim hooked to the queen. He believed that it was pulling life from the queen, but there was also a return element of death magic. Melikin was sure that if he severed, the link the queen would be killed. He also theorized that if he killed the queen, Al-Shaim would starve. Melikin wrote a question at the bottom of the page. "Would the tomb survive the queen's death?"

I was turning the page when I heard footsteps coming back down the steps. Samantha was yelling, "We have to go! The tomb is failing! Come quick, Wess!"

I jumped up and ran for the steps. As soon as she saw me coming, she turned and began running back up. I chugged up the stairs as fast as I could, but she was pulling away from me. After four more flights, I heard her running down a hallway above me. She was yelling something, but she was too far ahead, and the sound was bouncing off the walls.

I finally made the hallway and saw her turn into another room at the end of the hall. She had both her swords drawn, and there was a bright red light coming from the room. I ran down the hall and turned into the room. Samantha stood in front of a large, black glass, egg-shaped coffin that had swirling red clouds twisting angrily inside of it. The glass was cracking as I watched and light was pouring from the cracks, casting strange crimson shadows around the room.

I held Azurain in front of me and looked with my gift. There was a solid red tether going from the top of the coffin up through the ceiling and a very slight green link pulsed back along it. I walked up beside Samantha and asked, "Is your mother in the room above us?"

Samantha nodded and said, "Yes, but she is barely hanging on. I suspect the walls are falling now."

"Al-Shaim has been draining her slowly for years, but now he has no need for secrecy. He is pulling harder now that he knows we are coming for him. If we kill Al-Shaim, do the zombies all die?" I asked.

She looked at me with concern and shrugged, "I don't know."

"Well, I don't see any energy going out to them from Al-Shaim, so I don't think so. We may have to deal with them after we deal with him," I said.

"Without fire, that will be difficult. You can cut them in half and they keep coming. If my magic was stronger, I could take my people back through the portal, but it takes all my will just to transport me. Even Larissa can only take one other. I don't know how we will protect everyone."

I looked up at the green strand and knew it was almost spent. It was just a thread now. I whispered, "Be ready Samantha, your mother is almost gone."

Even as I finished warning her, the cracks in the coffin widened. Suddenly, little writhing tendrils of red colored death magic started flailing toward Samantha. I lashed out with Azurain as one got close to her. It cut cleanly through it and the energy dispersed in front of her. The tendrils pulled back quickly, and there was a large pulse that shot out the top and through the roof. As it passed through, the green energy pulsed once in response then was no more. I was sure I had just watched the queen be killed with a large burst of death magic. Right after the green flow from the roof shut off, the red flow from the coffin stopped as well.

Above us, somewhere in the palace, I heard a bell start to ring franticly. If the walls had just fallen. The dead would be pouring in. I hoped all the elves made it behind the barricade.

Samantha and I stood frozen, waiting for something to happen. As we watched, weapons ready, the black smoke leaked from the cracks. It snaked out around us and started filling the room. I looked at Samantha and I could see that she wore the same concerned expression that I did, but she made no move to flee.

The smoke billowed forth, and before long, the entire room filled with it. It had no smell but was so thick that I couldn't even see Samantha standing next to me. There was a bright flash in the smoke, and I felt a weird pulling sensation. I blinked, and when I opened my eyes, the smoke had cleared and we were standing in a different room. Samantha spun around looking for danger, and I did the same.

The room was a giant circle with corridors leading off in all directions. Grey stone lined the walls and weird domes of white glass lit the ceiling.

I heard the sound of bare feet coming toward us. I touched Samantha's shoulder and pointed in the direction I heard it. She moved quickly and quietly next to the opening and peered down it. I did the same, just not quite as gracefully. I felt like she moved as a cat would and I moved like dog...maybe a dog who hadn't grown into his paws yet.

I looked down the hall and was glad to see the glass light domes went in a perfect row along the ceiling. They illuminated a woman with white hair wearing a white silky bed robe shuffling toward us. Samantha's eyes went wide and she called out with a quivering voice, "Mother?"

The woman looked up, and I could see that it was the sunken face from the sphere I had seen. There was one major difference though: her eyes were open and glowing red. The queen let out a shriek, and I could see her mouth was full of pointy teeth. She raised her arms toward Samantha and started running toward her with a hungry look on her face. Samantha back pedaled into the room as her dead mother closed in on her with her arms outstretched.

Chapter 10: Mothers

My gift showed a thin red line trailing from the dead queen as she came charging into the room. Samantha was frozen, a look of horror on her face. I was in a little shock myself, but I knew if I didn't act something awful was about to happen to Samantha.

I stepped into my throw and released Azurain. I had to lead her a little because I was throwing from the side and she was running faster than a dead lady should be able to. My axe struck her in the side of the head, and she disappeared immediately, the red trail retracting down the hall rapidly. I ran to follow, Azurain appearing back in my hand as took up pursuit of the rapidly retreating strand.

I didn't wait for Samantha. I didn't want to lose track of the strand. The idea of trying to figure out where to go in all this maze of halls made me feel a sense of urgency. I ran as fast as I could, but the death magic flow was retracting much faster.

I reached out to connect to the natural energies and was surprised when I connected to energy from a living mushrooms all around me. I didn't have time to think about it and pictured myself as a cheetah. I had never tried this form before and had only seen this cat when the traveling menagerie had come to visit the castle when I was a kid. I probably got the spots wrong and I am sure that a real cheetah would have been unimpressed, but I was extremely happy when my speed increased dramatically as I dropped to all fours.

Ahead, I saw the red line retract around a corner, and I charged into another round room. My mother was standing in front of an open hallway across the room. She looked just as I had remembered her before she was taken, even the clothes she was wearing. I was so surprised that my concentration faltered, and I snapped back into my human form with the lapse. I was running at such a high speed that I tripped and slid across the room. My human legs were simply not meant to go that fast.

I got up as quick as I could and saw my mother with her arms open and a tear on her cheek. "My boy, it has been so long. I have missed you so, come give your mother a hug."

My heart broke, I thought about running to her. I missed my mother so badly, but I knew she couldn't be here. I shook my head and clutched my axe to my chest. I couldn't speak; the lump in my throat wouldn't allow it.

She stepped forward asking, "What's wrong, Wess, did you forget about me? Did you stop caring for me? Why won't you come hug me?"

I stepped back, finding my voice, "You are not my mother!"

She smiled warmly and took another step, "You are confused, Wess, of course I am your mother. Al-Shaim brought me here with his magic. He wants you to work with him in an alliance. Won't you come give me a hug? Please, Wess, you are breaking my heart!"

I felt tears running down my cheeks. I wanted to believe that this was my mother, but it couldn't be.

I gathered my resolve and spoke firmly, "You look well-fed, mother, too well fed for someone who has been held captive for more than a year. Nice try, Al-Shaim, but why don't you quit hiding behind projections of mothers and show yourself!"

Samantha came running into the room with her eyes wide and stopped next to me, whispering, "Wess, she looks like you."

I spoke loudly to the room, "Yes, Al-Shaim is a coward! He killed his own mother and now he tries to use ours against us. What's the matter, Al-Shaim? Never got over that, did you?"

My mother's face twisted in rage, a look I had never seen her make. My mother was kind and gentle. I was sure this wasn't her, but now I started to believe all of this was some sort of projection from Al-Shaim's twisted mind. My mother's face twisted and morphed and suddenly I was looking at the woman from the book. I was looking at Al-Shaim's mother.

She screamed at me. Her lips were moving, but I was hearing Al-Shaim's voice, "She hated me! I was never good enough for her! I was always a failure, even when I showed her what I could do! When I brought our dead dog back to life, she threw me out in the streets!"

Samantha and I shared a look, and I said, "This freak has some serious issues."

The mother figure in front of me shrieked and dove toward us. I didn't have time to pull my arm back so I flipped Azurain toward her underhanded and as it struck, she disappeared, just as the image of the queen had.

I willed Azurain back before it struck the wall behind her. I watched as the red death magic thread quickly receded down the hall again.

I turned to Samantha and spoke, "I am not sure what is going on here, but we are wasting time and I am tired of fighting on his terms."

She nodded, "I agree, but how do we draw him out? We could wander around these halls for hours, and in that time, the undead will be attacking my people."

"I don't know," I said, "but I am starting to think that is his plan. He means to delay us while he gathers a bigger army. I think this means that he is afraid to face us right now,"

The stone walls here were the first rock I had seen since we came through the Fae Gate. I reached out with my gift to see if I could connect to the stone elements. I was not surprised when I found no rock element there. I always felt connected to the stone in the castle. It didn't matter to my gift if stone was in the ground or cut into blocks, it worked the same either way. I walked to the wall and touched it with my fingers. It looked like stone, but it didn't feel right. I closed my eyes and ran my hand along it. I knew my hand was passing over joints, and I should be feeling the contours change beneath my fingers, but it all felt the same. It reminded me of the mushrooms that the houses were all carved out of.

Samantha grew impatient, "What are we doing Wess? We are wasting time!"

I held my hand up signaling for her to give me a moment more. I reached out with my gift and tried to only pull energy from the wall in front of me. I did this like it was a living thing, a giant mushroom to be precise. The mushroom responded and energy trickled into me. I cut it off and opened my eyes, looking into Samantha's.

"This isn't real, we are still in the palace. None of this stone is real, these walls are all mushroom! I don't think we have moved at all from the room with the coffin."

Samantha looked around confused, then poked her sword into the wall. It slid into the stone easily. She looked back to me, "How can that be? I thought we were entering another dimension? I thought we were being pulled into Al-Shaim's tomb?" she asked.

I responded, "I don't know, but maybe Al-Shaim's tomb is of his own making? I think this is all from his head."

I touched Azurain to the wall, and where I held it, the wall faded and I could see the mushroom wall behind it. As soon as I removed it, the wall appeared back. "His magic isn't strong enough to overcome another artifact," I said.

She nodded, and I turned in a circle trying to figure out a way to break out of this. I talked out loud just trying to think it through, "If we are still in that room then we weren't actually running. That room wasn't very large. That means we weren't physically transported anywhere right?"

Samantha nodded, "That makes sense. So, were you actually throwing Azurain in the real world?"

I looked down at my axe and nodded slowly, "I think so, maybe. When I threw Azurain, maybe it knew to cut the energy making that projection. I kept seeing a thin red energy tether that retracted each time I destroyed an image. Maybe Azurain isn't being fooled by all of this and it is reacting to my need to destroy the image of your mother and mine."

"So you need to get rid of the tether making all of this." She waived her sword at the room.

I nodded and spoke, "I will try, Samantha." I closed my eyes again and pictured the room as it was before the smoke filled it. I pictured where we were standing and the direction we were facing. I focused on the egg shaped coffin, and I pictured a red tendril coming from it hooked to me and Samantha. Without opening my eyes, I stepped forward and threw Azurain at the red tether and pictured it severing the connection to Al-Shaim that I was sure was there. It was an easy throw in my head, and I heard the familiar whomp sound and fell onto my butt. My eyes flew open to see that we were back in the room with the coffin. There was no smoke, but I saw Azurain embedded in the ground next to the coffin and a thick red tether retracting into the glass egg.

Samantha was first up and she spun quickly, both blades flashed out, and she cut the arms off a zombie who had just walked into our room. I willed Azurain to my hand and turned to face the new threat.

My heart dropped into my stomach. Behind the zombie Samantha had dis-armed were at least thirty more, and a steady stream were stalking up the stairs behind them. Samantha jammed her boot into the chest of the zombie and it went flying backward into the one behind it.

I threw Azurain sideways, the blade spun right through the neck of the zombie who caught the stumbler. Azurain appeared back in my hand as the headless zombie kept staggering toward us.

Samantha screamed, "I will hold them back! You must destroy Al-Shaim!"

Samantha spun into the crowd of undead and I couldn't help but be impressed as legs and arms flew off everywhere she went. Ben was all power and direct force, but Samantha was pure efficiency and grace. Every move set up the next three. Her blades were a blur, and I had to shake myself to stop watching her fluid movements.

I turned back toward the coffin in time to swipe away a death tendril wiggling toward me. It yanked back as Azurain passed through it.

I knew I needed to act quickly. As good as Samantha was, eventually the zombies would overwhelm her. I leapt up on the coffin and swung down on the glass with both hands gripping my axe. The blade bit deep and stuck in the shell. Instead of trying to pry it free, I stood up and willed it back to my hand. Azurain complied as I swung down again. I turned my strike a little to cross the gash I had just made. Once again the artifact's blade bit into the glass, but this was going to be slow work. I attacked the casket again, but the snakelike approach of another tendril forced my attention to it instead. Azurain slashed through it, and the stem recoiled.

I heard Samantha's strained voice from the hall, "Hurry please, Wess!"

I knew I didn't have time to keep hacking at this thing. Azurain had changed its blade shape for me before based on my need. I knew it had been a sword for Nelzeroth and a staff for Rissling.

I focused all of my need on Azurain and lifted it straight up above the glass. A flash of red came from my left, but I ignored it and drove my axe handle straight down instead. My axe blade pulled back and my curved handle straightened, lengthening into a smooth shaft. Right before impact a long spear blade shot out as I drove it down between my feet with all my force. The blade drove right through the crack I had made. I felt Azurain pass through the glass and strike something solid underneath.

There was a massive explosion from inside and the glass shattered outward. I was launched through the air and smashed into the wall, pain lancing through me from a hundred cuts. I slid down the wall and started flowing healing energy through my cuts. I was greeted by new pain as my body forced glass shards from fresh wounds. I stood and stumbled back toward the pedestal that held the coffin. Azurain had passed straight through the chest of Al-Shaim and was embedded in the mushroom floor beneath the coffin. I willed it back to my hand as I staggered to the body.

A piece of glass fell from my knee, and suddenly I could walk correctly, the stabbing I had felt melting away as the healing energies borrowed from the earth closed the wound.

Al-Shaim had a pained expression frozen on his shriveled face. It seemed that his four hundred year entombment had an effect on him just as it did the queen. Crimsura's red runes pulsed as I gazed down on him. I remembered that Sevest had instructed me not to touch it, and now that I knew it worked like Azurain, it made sense. If I touched it, I would be bound to it until I was dead. I quickly took the bag off my belt and put my hand through it, snatching the red torque from Al-Shaim's body.

Samantha backed into the room, zombies staggering after. She stopped at the door, her flashing blades keeping them from entering. "You okay, Wess?" she called over her shoulder.

I ran up behind her and said, "Yes, Al-Shaim is dead and I have Crimsura in this bag. How do we get out of here?" I held up the bag to show her.

She glanced back toward me while hacking the hand off a slow moving corpse. "Only one way I can think of!"

Her other blade flashed toward me as she spun. The blade sliced easily through the bottom of the bag and Crimsura dropped from the bottom. Her spin continued and she dropped her first blade, catching the torque with her bare right hand.

I shouted out in despair, but it came out as some kind of gurgling choking sound. I was too shocked to react as the torque turned into a liquid form, poured down her hand and wrapped itself around Samantha's wrist, forming a bracelet.

Zombies piled into the room falling on top of her. She dropped her other sword and grabbed my ankle. I swung

Azurain in a sideways arc and chopped another zombies head off, but before it hit the ground I felt energy course up through my leg and the room changed instantly.

Suddenly, we were in the in the great hall surrounded by battle ready elves. All of them were armored and armed and looking surprised to see us. The openings into the room were choked with zombie corpses. Elves were busy hacking them and throwing them back into the hall.

Samantha shouted, "To me! To me! Quickly!"

I couldn't stop looking at the red runes on the bracelet, I was trying to puzzle through what this would mean for my mother.

The elves responded immediately and several hundred of them rushed toward us. Samantha leapt up on a mushroom bench and yelled, "Everyone touch someone else! Hurry, we are going home!"

The elves swarmed in, followed by a host of zombies. Samantha grabbed two elves and closed her eyes. Dejectedly, I grabbed the hand of an older female elf next to me and once again, I felt Samantha's energy flow through me as the entire room changed.

Sunlight filtered through tall trees. We were outside standing in the shade of the giant tree I had come through originally. Everyone wore shocked or confused looks. Suddenly, they burst into excited hooting, jumping, and spinning. The old woman next to me grabbed my face and kissed me full on the lips.

She pulled back from me and said, "Oh if I was seven hundred years younger!"

She twirled off as I stood there with my mouth hanging open.

Samantha walked toward me, smiling with unbound joy. She took both my hands and whispered, "We did it, Wess. We saved my people and brought them home! Be happy Wess, you have done a marvelous thing today. Elves will sing your name for centuries to come."

I couldn't meet her eyes. I looked around at the elves dancing and celebrating, "I promised Sevest that I would exchange Crimsura for my mother's freedom, Samantha. He will not be pleased by this and the Druids only gave me ten days to rescue her. I don't know what I will do now."

She crossed her arms and said, "I see. I'm sorry, Wess, I wasn't aware of all that. It wouldn't have changed my actions though. This was our only way out, and I wouldn't have traded all of my people for your mother."

I nodded, "I know. You're right. I wouldn't have either. I just don't know what to do now."

"Well, tonight we will feast and celebrate. The elves will start to build a home here, and in the morning, you and I will go talk to Sevest together. We have two of the artifacts. If we work together, we can do anything," she said enthusiastically.

Chapter 11: Elf-home

One thing I will say about elves that have been trapped in a land of eternal night surrounded by undead for four hundred years: they knew how to party! The smell of roasted stag drifted past me as I drank the unfermented mulberry. Everyone else was drinking the mulberry wine that I had fermented with my druid powers. It was Samantha's idea. Once she had explained to me what needed to happen it was easy enough. I grew thousands of juicy berries, which the elves squished into barrels that I formed for them out of dead wood.

It took a little experimentation, but Samantha didn't seem to mind sipping each one and telling me what to do to it. She would add some yellow powder and have me accelerate its growth. The powder was called yeast and apparently it drank the berry juice and pee'd out wine. Without me Samantha said the process would take months, but a little earth energy made the yeast go crazy. The barrels foamed and bubbled whenever I made the yeast grow faster. I decided right then I was never going to be a big wine drinker.

Samantha seemed thrilled with the process. Once we got it right she kissed me on the cheek and twirled around with her cup held high. She said it wasn't ice wine, but after all this time she thought everyone would be very happy with it. I was just happy to make her so happy.

After making the wine, I set about the task of forming the things the elves would need to survive. I made plates and cups and found several springs of water nearby. I formed barrels and filled them with the spring water. That part was fun. I had it shoot up and arc into the bucket. Lastly, I formed a lute, a flute, and a set of drums that an elf stretched some buckskin over. I was careful not to pull too much energy and I pulled a tiny amount from a wide area so I wouldn't hurt one plant too much. It was fun to use my powers to help the elves, and after four hundred years I felt like they deserved it.

My last act was to weave a great hall out of vines. I formed walls and anchored each corner to a large tree. I formed the roof with overlapping leaves so that if it rained, the water would trickle down and out from the middle. I finished by growing long tables and benches around three fire pits in the middle. The elves stacked piles of wood and turned a deer carcass over each one. As the light faded, I sat at one of these benches and savored the smell of the roasting meat.

The elves started playing music. They were a joyful bunch to watch. Everyone was singing and dancing to the music, spinning around the hall. I was doing well going unnoticed but finally a giggling elf maiden came bouncing up to me and dragged me off the bench. I was trying to say no, but her energy was contagious. Before I knew it, we were twirling around with the other elves. I was passed off to several partners through the night and did my best not to step on anyone's toes. I had to admit it was fun. Everyone was so happy that I couldn't help but be happy too.

After a couple hours, I finally managed to sit and eat, exhausted from all the dancing. Samantha came over with a plate and a cup of wine. She sat in front of me smiling. She had a rosy blush to her cheeks and I was sure that was not her first cup this evening.

"Hey Wess, you having fun?" she asked with a slight giggle.

I couldn't help but smile, "I have to admit that I am having fun. I wish I was better at dancing."

She giggled again, "Oh you did just fine. I think Twincy likes you!" She pointed out the young elven girl that had originally asked me to dance, then she added, "She is young like you. She is only forty three."

I snorted and the mulberry juice came out my nose. I laughed and wiped it on my sleeve, "Umm, I am twelve. No, wait, what is today? My birthday is day two hundred and sixty one."

Her eyes went wide, "That was yesterday! Happy birthday, Wess! Wow, you are only thirteen? You look at least thirty five or forty!"

Suddenly, the music stopped and the elves parted. I looked over at the entrance and saw an unusually large bear that I knew right away. I jumped up and ran toward her shouting, "Hannah Bear!"

She roared and stood on her hind legs as I crashed into her. She hugged me tight and made a happy growling noise. I backed up and let her come back down on all fours. I scratched her under her spiked collar, and she pressed her forehead into my chest.

Samantha spoke behind me, "You know this bear?"

I nodded, "Yeah, she kind of adopted me as a cub, and she helped me escape from Rissling. I guess we helped each other as I freed her from the arena too."

She giggled a little, then shook her head and said, "Well, now it all makes sense. I was here a couple weeks ago and met this bear. She was traveling with an ogre. I confronted the ogre and we had a long conversation about you. The bear stayed here, and the ogre said he had to go join the bad army, but he was good."

"Wait, you had a long conversation with Ben?" I asked.

"Well, I asked a lot of questions, and he gave me one word answers. The ogre has a name?"

I answered, "Yes, actually he is a half-ogre. His name is Ben, he is my friend, too."

She stood there with her hands on her hips and said, "There is an old human expression that goes, 'you can tell a lot about a man by the company he keeps.' Your friends, while strange, seem loyal to you. Bring your bear in; she is welcome here. You will always be able to count the elves among your friends, Wess, and your friends will always be welcome no matter how strange."

Hannah followed me back to my table, but I was more comfortable sitting on the ground with her. One of the elves brought her a haunch of meat and she tore into it happily. I laid back against her as the music started up again. Her fur was soft, the music slow, and I had a full stomach. It didn't take me long to drift off into a lazy slumber.

I slept a deep dreamless sleep that I only get when I am exhausted. I awoke the next morning with a chill, still lying on Hannah Bear, but covered in morning dew and shivering. I walked to the fire pit, quietly weaving around sleeping elves. I uncovered the embers and blew on them until they flamed up and then added a few more logs.

I stood there warming myself and trying to wake up. Samantha walked up next to me looking wide awake and ready to go. I noticed she had replaced her swords. "So, how do we get to this Sevest person?" she asked.

I lifted my hand and showed her my ring, saying, "He gave me this ring to return to him once I had the torque. If I turn it to the right, I will teleport to him."

She nodded, then said, "I have seen these rings before. They are quite popular with Kurzak nobility."

It was my turn to nod, and I put my hand back over the fire. "Sevest isn't nobility, he is a creation of Rissling's, like Ben. He is part tiger and part man. He is very intriguing actually, he knows everything about what other people are doing. He scares me to be honest and I am not looking forward to disappointing him. I have a feeling that people who disappoint Sevest don't remain healthy for long."

She responded, "Hmm, I see. A creation of Rissling's? I assume this is the same Rissling who invaded Faermont? This was the one who had your mother, yes?"

I nodded, lost in the flames.

"Well, then I suppose we should be on our way," she said.

She took my shoulders and turned me to her and hugged me. She whispered in my ear, "I am with you, Wess; we will do what it takes."

I stepped back from her and asked, "How will we get there together?"

She took my hand and looked at the ring again, "I have a theory. My gift allows me to trigger the gates or to teleport to somewhere I am familiar with. I am hoping that I can use the ring to transport us both. With Crimsura augmenting my power, I think I can manage it. Will you let me try?"

I took the ring off and handed it to her. She put it on her thumb, which I thought was odd, but it seemed to fit her well. She drew one of her swords with her right hand and took my hand with her left. She looked at me, and I nodded. This is when she showed me that putting it on her thumb was no accident: its placement there allowed her to turn the ring and wield a sword at the same time. She lifted that sword into the air, rolled her thumb up, and twisted the ring to the right.

There was a flash of darkness like I blinked, and everything changed in an instant. We were no longer in a forest. We were now in the courtyard of a large estate. Standing in front of us, or kind of standing, were two creatures with snake heads, muscular human torsos, and long, thick snake bodies. They were well-armored and appeared ready for battle. They casually held spears at an angle across their chests as they stood in front of a wide marble staircase that led up to an elegant, two-story home.

We both jumped suddenly as Sevest spoke right behind us, almost in our ears, "Well, I wasn't expecting you to bring a guest, Wess."

Chapter 12: Barter

Samantha dropped my hand, stepped away from Sevest and turned to allow her to see the snake guards and him. I did the same, but turned in the other direction.

Sevest spread his hands to show he meant no harm. He purred, "Such a pretty guest! Wess, you certainly know how to get a job done! I ask you to bring me an ancient artifact and you bring me a beautiful elf maiden wearing it. I do say that you know how to go above and beyond in the performance of a task! Would you and Samantha care to come inside?"

Samantha did not look pleased and asked, "I don't believe we have been introduced, do I know you, cat?"

Sevest gave a toothy grin, which I have to say was impressive since he had fangs. "We have not been introduced, my lady. I am Sevest, minor lord of this house and uninitiated member of the fourth circle of Kurzak nobility." With that, he bowed formally.

Samantha scowled, and Sevest continued, "I presume that you are Sae-Sauril-Eloeen, known by your human name, Samantha, Elf Queen and Elven Protectorate."

Samantha looked very surprised now, and her sword point lowered as she spoke, "I am not queen yet."

Sevest did a little flick motion with his hand and said, "A formality. Your people will insist, and you, of course, will say yes. They have looked to you for leadership for four hundred years. You will not let them down when they are beginning this new chapter in their lives. Now, please let us go to my solarium, I have iced wine and fruit prepared. This Kurzak sun drains me so."

He stepped forward and offered us each a paw. We looked at one another, then each took one. Once again, there was a flash of darkness and our scene changed. We now stood in a room with a small, well-polished coffee table, a love seat, and two chairs. Sevest picked up a small silver bell and rang it. Two young women came in with silver trays and set out fruit and three goblets on the table, then quickly left.

Sevest sat on the love seat. Samantha unhooked her sword belt and draped it over the high-backed chair. I sat in the chair closest to the door and helped myself to some fruit. As usual, I was starving.

Sevest picked up his wine as Samantha was sitting down and said, "It seems we have a conundrum." He looked at me and asked, "Do you know what that means, Wess?"

I looked up with an orange slice in my mouth. I smiled sheepishly so that it looked like I had a big orange smile. Sevest just stared at me, so I spit out the rind and swallowed the fruit. "Um, I am guessing it means a problem?"

Sevest nodded, "Well I like to think of it as a challenge, but yes, we do have a problem I suppose. You see, I have already begun working to free your mother in good faith, as we agreed. I did this at considerable risk to myself and my house. As it turns out, you will not be able to live up to your side of the bargain after all. I am assuming that you will not be killing Samantha here so that you may complete our transaction?"

I swallowed a grape and shook my head, "No, I was hoping we could alter our agreement. Is there something else we could do in exchange for my mother's freedom?"

Sevest turned his head and gazed out the window. He sat there for a while with a far-away look on his face, and I started to fidget. The tall chair wasn't that comfortable, and I had a lot of nervous energy. Samantha looked at me and placed her hand on mine. I remembered what she had told me. I released the energy, calming myself and slowing my heart beat.

Sevest turned back to us and said, "I must consider the options. Your mother's removal from Rissling's house will be happening tonight. I would like some time to consider what I want from you two since Crimsura is out of my reach now. Is this acceptable to you?"

Samantha and I looked at each other and nodded. "Sure." I said, "That sounds fair."

"Oh good, I am so glad that everyone is being so reasonable. I am sure we can come to an agreement on a fair exchange of services."

He stood and we did as well, then he added almost as an afterthought, "Samantha, just so I am clear in my understanding of your agreement with me: since you are the reason that Wess will not be able to live up to his agreement, you are now offering your services in addition to his, in some agreed upon action? Do I understand that correctly?"

Samantha and I shared a look; I was sure she was feeling the corner we were being backed into as well. Samantha looked back to Sevest and answered cautiously, "Yes, I suppose that's correct. I am here to help Wess fulfill his agreement."

"Very good, I would hate to think that Wess or the new Queen of the Elves wouldn't live up to their word," Sevest said smoothly as he walked to the door. He opened it and gestured for us to go out.

I felt unsettled about what Sevest would propose next, but I couldn't really see a way out of it at this point. We didn't have anything to offer. We moved into the foyer then followed Sevest out into the courtyard.

He stopped in front of two more serpent guards at the white brick wall and turned to speak to us, "Wess, you are a wanted man here, but there aren't too many who know what you look like. Even so, it would not behoove me to be seen with you, so I would ask that you wear this hat."

Sevest reached back behind him and pulled out a floppy hat and plopped it on my head. I couldn't see where the hat had come from; it was like it appeared from inside his cloak.

Samantha started giggling almost immediately and covered her mouth with her hand.

"Is the hat that bad?" I asked.

Samantha was still giggling, and she shook her head no, answering, "It isn't the hat. It's the illusion. You look like an old woman!"

My eyes went wide and I touched my own face, which made Sevest shake his head. "It doesn't actually turn you into an old woman Wess, just makes you look like one," he said.

I shrugged and laughed a little myself before responding, "Well, as long as I don't smell like one!"

I laughed at my own joke and as I did I turned and faced the serpent headed guard. It stood there and flicked its tongue at me, completely unimpressed with my humor. I didn't know how a snake would look if it smiled and apparently I wasn't going to find out today.

We walked out of the gate, and I was entirely unprepared for what I saw. Kurzak was remarkably different from

Swansea. Swansea was all low buildings built around a castle on a hill. The entire city had an orderly semblance of small leading up to large, farms on the outside and dense taller buildings closer to the castle.

Kurzak, the capital city of the nation of Kurzak was stunning in its differences. We walked out onto a paved road that was wider than any I had ever been on. Across from Sevest's estate was another walled estate. This one was a massive pyramid shape, but it stepped up on each level. That one estate could have held six of Sevest's, but it wasn't even close to being the largest. On the outside of the massive gate was the yellow symbol that I had seen all the Grelkin wear on their chests. I turned back to Sevest's gate as it swung closed and saw a painting of a tiger's head on his gate. I looked around at the street and except for a few cloaked figures, it was mostly empty.

Sevest stood patiently and watched Samantha and I as we took it all in. I finally turned to him and asked, "Is that Rissling's estate there?"

Sevest nodded, "Yes, Rissling lives in the Ziggurat. I believe in the old axiom *keep your friends close and your enemies closer*. When I moved in across the street from Rissling, it almost started a war between our houses. He was not happy with me when I forced him to grant my freedom, but even less so when I became his neighbor by choice."

Sevest started walking slowly up the street, and I asked another question, "That symbol on Rissling's gate, does it mean something?"

Sevest nodded, "All of the major noble houses use sorcerous symbols as their standard. Rissling's is the first symbol, it means he has only mastered the creation of grelkin."

"Peace." Samantha said with a far-away look.

Sevest and I both looked at her expectantly.

She elaborated, "It was the symbol for peace, thousands of years ago."

Sevest shrugged, "Well, there's nothing peaceful about it now; that is certain. Once he manages a more difficult creature, he will gain other symbols. The highest houses have all nine symbols. For houses such as myself, I have mine, with no one on my staff with sorcerous abilities, I must purchase my guards from the She-ur-ar. Those are sorcerers who have chosen not align themselves with a particular house."

As we walked on, the estates varied in sizes, but one thing remained the same: they were all walled and guarded. Sevest turned left down a street that was just as large as the one before.

"Sevest, where are the market, the inns, and places like that?" I asked.

Sevest stopped and turned to us, "Kurzak is not like other towns you have been. No one trusts anyone here. Each estate is self-sufficient and relies only on itself. The larger estates have magic gateways to communities that keep them supplied with food, materials, and slaves for their experiments. The smaller estates rely on guilds to deliver everything they need."

Sevest pointed to a low walled estate, the buildings so short that I could just see the tips of a few roofs peaking over. The sounds of metal on metal rang out from inside. On the gate was a symbol of a hammer. He said, "That symbol is for the blacksmith's guild. They supply those estates that don't have the abilities to create their own armor and weapons. If you need their services, you make an appointment and meet inside their walls."

Samantha spoke then, "This place really isn't set up for visitors, is it?"

Sevest shook his head, "No one visits here. A visitor is just a slave that hasn't been captured yet. Anyone not of a house is a slave. I show you all of this so you understand what we are up against. The entire culture of slavery will have to change here."

Samantha frowned, "There is no word for slave in Elvish. The idea is truly repugnant."

Sevest turned to her and said, "My lady, I could not agree more. Alas, I do not know how it would be possible to bring about such a positive change here, but having been a slave myself, I would do it if it were in my power. They do not respect slaves here and treat them as nothing more than property. I have seen houses experiment on them, torture, and kill them for their entertainment. They justify it all by deciding that slaves are some lower form of life. They aren't even considered human and no Kurzak law protects them."

I didn't trust Sevest yet, but I felt like he was telling the truth about this. I thought about his response for a moment then asked, "How did you achieve freedom then?"

Sevest grinned again, and I couldn't help but step back half a step. I felt like I was a steak. If he licked his lips I would have started running. Finally, he looked off down the street as if remembering and answered me, "Rissling is the lord of a small house, and I worked my way into his confidence. I crafted a plan for him to gain a magical formula from a greater house. I stole the spell and materials for half-ogres, but in doing so, I planted evidence against Rissling. This evidence is hidden in the house of the other lord. If it were ever discovered, it would start a war and Rissling would likely be crushed. I used this leverage to barter for my freedom."

Sevest stood there for a while staring off down the street and Samantha and I shared a look. Sevest would be a difficult adversary. Then he added, "I have connections with the slaves of all the major houses. I was going to use Crimsura to begin a revolution. I had hoped that it would grant me enough power to overthrow the twelve lords of Kurzak, including Lord Algrier. I would have ended slavery here forever."

Sevest turned back to me, and I jumped at the opportunity, "Samantha and I could do it!"

Sevest and Samantha were both shaking their heads, but Sevest responded, "Even if you succeeded, I couldn't hold any authority without power. These lords only respect strength. The moment you went back to your homelands, they would rebel against me. Such a large change would require me to completely dominate them."

Samantha spoke next, "There were seven artifacts, what if we could find another one?"

Sevest stared at her for a moment, "Do you know where any of them are?"

Samantha shook her head and said, "I don't, but maybe the keepers of the great library of Gress do. It is not close to here, but if we could get there maybe they would have knowledge of one of the other five."

Sevest looked at us both then said, "You have my agreement. If you bring me an unbound artifact and help me overthrow the lords of Kurzak, your part of the agreement will be fulfilled. Slavery will be abolished in Kurzak."

Sevest took us back to his estate by a different route and showed us Lord Algrier's compound. I couldn't see past the black polished walls, but outside were two muscled guards with the heads of dragons. We observed them from the corner as Sevest spoke, "See the nine symbols on the gate?"

I nodded. They were chiseled into the gate, so they were actually tough to see, but now that he pointed them out, I could see they were there in a neat little line.

He continued, "You should also notice that his guards are on the outside of the walls. Only the major lords do that and I have to say that Lord Algrier's guards are some of the most impressive. The Kurzak gather once a year to watch their champions battle to the death. Lord Algrier's has won the past three year's melee quite easily. As a reward, Lord Algrier feeds his champion a young slave he wins from the defeated house."

"Does he have one of his dragons fight?" I asked. Having fought one I could see how they would be difficult to beat.

Sevest responded, "Actually, the rules of the melee require the creature to be half human. This way the lords can control them with the linking stones."

I looked at Samantha, and she looked as confused as me. It reassured me that I wasn't a complete moron for asking my next question, "Sevest, what's a linking stone?"

Sevest looked at me, then Samantha, and then responded, "Ah sorry, everyone from here knows about these things. The sorcerers use the linking stones to control their creations. The stones are part of the magical creation process. For each creature type, they create a linking stone that allows the sorcerer to maintain control of that creature. They don't bother when they are testing a new breed, but once they are ready to make them into guards or troops they always create a linking stone. I was a one of a kind, and Rissling considers me a mistake, since I went against him."

Samantha asked, "Why wouldn't Rissling create a linking stone for you now?"

Sevest shook his head, "It doesn't work that way, it must be done through the creation process. During the spell casting, the sorcerer puts some of their aspect and some of the creature's into a gem stone. Weaker willed creatures require smaller, less precious gems. One grelkin, for instance, might require a chip of topaz. You can bind thousands of grelkin into a single diamond. The linking stone is somehow absorbed into the sorcerer during the process."

"Wait, like you mean they eat it or something?" I asked.

Sevest shrugged, "I don't know. It is a closely guarded secret and one I have never witnessed. I do know that they are limited in how many stones they can manage."

Sevest looked up to check the time and said, "It is nearing high sun. We should get you two under way. It is several days to the Library of Gress."

As we began walking again, Sevest said, "You should also be aware that all the estates around this one are sworn to serve Lord Algrier, including Rissling. There are eleven minor lords in his service, Rissling's estate is actually connected to the back wall of Lord Algrier's. When we move against him, we must be prepared to move against them all."

I stared at the tall black walls as we walked past and tried to envision what we would face during an assault on this place. Even with three artifacts, I wasn't sure we would be able to handle it, especially if the eleven other lords got involved. I pictured hundreds of the dragon-headed guards behind the walls all waiting for us. I was nervous about our chances and this was one major lord. If we were going to wipe out slavery for good, we would need to conquer all the major lords in Kurzak.

We arrived back at the estate and were served lunch as Sevest and Samantha looked at maps. Samantha had a theory that she could use her gift, augmented by Crimsura, to travel to a nearby Fae gate. After looking at the map, she thought she knew of one near the library.

For lunch Sevest consumed a raw steak and Samantha had a salad, I was served something called a cheeseburger. It was pretty much the best thing I have ever eaten, and I was so excited about it that Sevest had the cook come out to teach me how he made it. If I got nothing else from this experience, I decided then and there I would learn to cook. One day, I hoped to be able to make my own cheeseburger.

After we finished eating and we were preparing to go, I asked Sevest, "So, do you always eat raw meat?"

Sevest got that unnerving grin of his and said, "Oh yes, cooked meat is quite disgusting to me."

"And what kind of meats do you eat exactly?" I asked.

Sevest didn't answer he just looked at me like I was the steak. Samantha broke the silence and said, "All right, time to go." She held out her hand to me.

I took her hand, and Sevest said, "Oh, you should be aware that Rissling recently ordered enough materials to create an army of half-ogres and my spies report he is busy looking for an artifact himself."

Samantha and I looked at each other, both of us sharing the same thought, "Then we have no time to waste," she said.

Once again the darkness-blink thing happened, and we were suddenly in a forest, standing in the middle of a ring of mushrooms. In the distance, I heard what sounded like an elephant trumpet. I couldn't resist. I covered my mouth and said, "Excuse me, cheeseburgers make me gassy!"

Samantha tried to look all serious, but she finally cracked a smile. "You are such a doof, I can't believe the universe has selected you as a hero," she said while shaking her head and walking off. She was walking away from the elephant sound. "The library is this way," she called back to me.

As I followed her I said, "So this artifact enhances all my powers. I wonder if it would make my farts super smelly. Who knows, maybe that could be a new weapon for me?"

Samantha looked down at her arm and said, "Let's hope not, because I would cut off my own arm if that were the case."

I replied, "I wouldn't recommend it. I can tell you that it hurts a lot and makes eating really difficult."

She looked at me then with raised eyebrows and then looked at my hand. "Oh, I got a new one," I said, wiggling my fingers.

She looked confused and was going to ask another question, but then we came out of the line of trees and saw the library, or what was left of it. Samantha broke into a run when she saw the large stone doors to the library had been knocked inwards. I ran to follow, and connected to the natural energies, scanning the surroundings for anything dangerous. I looked back to the library in time to see Samantha disappear and reappear right by the door still running full speed. She quickly entered the doorway ahead of me.

Since there was no fae gate at the door, I was guessing that Samantha just discovered that she could teleport anywhere she was looking. It took me another ten seconds to get to the door, and I had time to see blood and a body just inside the door. The building was a single long and narrow two-story stone structure with a pointed 'A' shape and two large, stone columns out front. Entering the building, I could see that this body wasn't the only one. Monks wearing brown robes lay dead in a line against the wall to the right.

When I entered fully, I saw that Samantha was facing three ogres; two more ogres lay dead behind her. Before I could react, one of them swung a club at her. She dove under it, rolled through its legs, and sliced outwards cutting across the back of the ogre's knees. It collapsed, wailing and grabbing the back of its legs.

I armored myself in stone and started running across the room. The other two ogres swung down hard with their clubs, and I thought I was about to watch Samantha be pulverized. The clubs struck stone as Samantha disappeared and suddenly reappeared behind the ogre on the right. Before he could regain his balance, the tips of Samantha's two swords erupted from his chest. The ogre looked confused by the metal points protruding from his body, then he fell dead.

Samantha smiled wickedly at her last opponent as she stepped onto the dead ogre to yank her swords out. I arrived then, but Samantha wasn't waiting for me. She drove in as the final ogre backpedaled, her blades flashing so fast I couldn't follow them. Within seconds, the ogre had dropped his club and clutched at its throat as blood spilled freely down its arm.

The ogre with the injured legs was trying to stand back up and had made it to his knees. Samantha spun without hesitation and struck the creature's neck with her lead sword. The ogre's huge head flew from it shoulders and struck me in my armored rock chest before dropping to my feet. I looked down to see that the ogre wore a shocked look on its decapitated face. As I dropped my rock form, I was sure my face looked about the same.

I looked up at Samantha, and she was already cleaning and sheathing her swords. I had fought her before, but with Crimsura on her arm she was faster than I thought anyone could move. She also seemed to be able to teleport at will now. When she looked at me finally, I said, "I am glad you are on my side, you're kinda awesome now."

She smiled and seemed pleased with her new abilities. She asked, "Any of the monks alive?"

I closed my eyes and reached out with my gift. There was no sign of life from the monks next to us, but I felt a spark from the back of the room. It was faint and wasn't at ground level. I opened my eyes and pointed at the balcony at the back of the room. "Up th..." Samantha grabbed my shoulder and we were suddenly on the balcony standing next to a dying monk.

"ere," I finished, but now I was pointing at some books right in front of me.

I sighed and bent to the monk. Samantha was clearly exceedingly happy with her new artifact. I couldn't blame her; I remembered myself dancing around in the woods making flowers not that long ago.

I put both my hands on the monk and felt his injuries. He had broken ribs and his lungs were collapsed. He was bleeding internally from a place where his ribs had jammed into other organs. I healed it all easily with borrowed energy from the nearby forest. His breathing became steady and his eyes fluttered open. I put a little regenerative energy into him to fix the blood loss and helped him to stand.

He appeared confused as he looked at us and ran his hand up and down his chest. A tear came to his eye, and he covered his mouth with his hand when he saw the bodies of his brothers.

He spoke, "I was standing by the doors when the ogres came in. The first one hit me with a club so hard I flew up here. I laid up here dying as the sorcerer killed my brothers one by one. Even after he got what he wanted, he killed them all."

Samantha growled, "Rissling." Then she asked gently, "What did the monks tell him?"

He tuned to her, "You know this evil man?" His tone turned hard and suspicious.

She looked to me and I lifted Azurain. His eyes went wide as he recognized my weapon. Samantha lifted her wrist, and I thought he was going to faint. Finally he said, "Never in my life did I think I should see one of the seven and now I am presented with two. I would not see this man Rissling get one."

Samantha spoke, "Help us stop him."

The monk looked again at his friends lying dead next to the ogres. "I will tell you everything I know about the seven, which is more than Rissling got from my brothers. It may give you an advantage," he said.

I shook my head, "We don't have time for you to tell us about all of them, we need to catch Rissling before he gets to the artifact."

The monk nodded, "Rissling was after Ambress; he came with some knowledge of its last known location. It has been missing for more than six hundred years."

He took a breath, considering where to start. He continued, "Ambress was used by a sorcerer named Alawaice."

I asked, "Does Rissling know this?"

The monk nodded, "He came asking about the nature of the demon guarding the treasure and the types of traps in the dungeon. He gained the information by torturing my brothers, but they claimed they didn't know what the creature is."

"But you know?" Samantha asked while pushing her hair behind her pointed ear.

"Yes. The creature is a powerful demon, summoned and bound by Alawaice to guard his wealth and his secrets almost six hundred years ago. The demon is known, in this realm, by the name Jerzatu and he has added defenses and traps to the dungeon for more than five hundred years since Alawaice died."

He took a deep breath then said, "Rissling will go to the tomb's well known entrance in the ruins of the sorcerer's keep. I would recommend that you go through the sewers of the nearby city of Answar." He pointed to a section of maps on the first floor. "I have maps to the city there and can describe how to get into the dungeon from below. You may be able to beat him there, but as for destroying Jerzatu, I can offer no sound advice. Many have tried, but all have failed."

I looked at Samantha and then the monk and shrugged, "Should be a breeze for Blink Girl and Nature Boy," I said.

Samantha grabbed my shoulder and the monk's and said, "If that name sticks, I will blink my sword right into your butt." With that, she blinked us down to the maps.

We appeared right where the monk pointed and he looked around before saying, "Well that is certainly handy!"

I nodded and responded, "Yeah, but I am worried that she will get fat now, since she is going to just go blinky blinky everywhere."

Samantha glared at me, and I looked to see if the monk thought it was funny, but he was staring at his dead friends with tears streaming down his cheeks. I looked to his friends and realized how insensitive I was being. I said, "Sir, would you allow me to bury your friends while you show Samantha the maps?" He nodded slightly, still in shock, and I added awkwardly, "Sorry about them." I wasn't very good at the grief thing.

I turned and fled the building to avoid crying in front of them. I walked to a small hill and used my gift to create four graves. The dirt moved from the ground easily and formed a neat pile next to the holes. Digging graves turned out to be one thing I was now really good at, but I didn't like doing.

I went back to the library and looked around. I felt like the dead ogres needed to go, but I couldn't see a way to move them. After some thought, I turned the floor to mud under each of them and let them sink into it. I had the water push their massive bodies lower before turning the floor solid again. This had the added benefit of removing most of the blood.

Next, I transformed into the rock element, growing twice my size and gaining strength from the stone underfoot. I stepped over to the dead monks and gently scooped two of them up and carried them outside. I went back for the other two and after I had placed one in each of the graves Samantha and the monk came outside. I dropped the rock form and stood patiently.

The monk shook my hand and said, "Not only have you saved my life today, but you have shown exceptional compassion. We have a saying in Fallis Chirch for close friends and family. 'My home is forever your home.' Please know that, for both of you, this is a literal statement. My name is Timothy Branch and if I can ever help in any way, you have but to ask it. Fallis Chirch is just over that rise. I have shown Samantha on the maps. If you ever need a bed or a meal, it is yours for the asking."

We thanked him and gave him our names as well, then we all stood there in silence for a while staring at the bodies. Timothy said some kind words about each of them as I covered them with the dirt. The grass grew back at my thought, and I felt a weird sense of peace wash over me as we stood there in silence.

Samantha and I said our goodbyes after some time, but before we teleported out, Timothy added one last thought, "Jerzatu has had hundreds of years to do nothing but improve his dungeon. If you are going to make it to the demon you will need to pass through the creations of a mind more devious than any human. You must think like a demon to have a chance. Good luck, my friends."

Chapter 14: Provisions

Samantha and I stared at the large stone tunnel that Timothy had guided us to. It was about six feet wide with two ledges above the trickle of water and sewage. I wasn't looking forward to entering the demon's dungeon, but the thought of walking in a tunnel full of sewage had me hoping we could get there quickly.

After teleporting to the closest Fae gate, we had already walked for almost half a day to arrive at this spot. The sun was about to dip below the horizon, casting the giant drain into darkness.

I muttered, "Hmm, I hadn't considered that it is going to be pitch black in there. I suppose we won't be so lucky as to find a frog that can see in the dark."

Samantha put her hand on her chin and considered me. I realized she had no idea what I was talking about. I tried to explain, "I can see through animals' eyes; I used a frog named Freddy to see in the dark once."

"I see," she said. "Even if you can change into an animal that can see or look through another animal's eyes, I do not like the idea that I would be blind. Maybe we should go above to the town of Answar and procure some lanterns and other supplies we might need."

I nodded and we began walking up the path on the side of the opening. I could picture kids coming down here to play even though their parents had forbidden it. I certainly would have, before I had constant adventure in my life. As I walked to the town, I considered the fact that since my parents had left, I really didn't play anymore; and since I got my powers I had been forced to grow up quickly. Every decision I made now seemed to have significant impacts on everyone around me and even people I didn't know.

Now I had entered into an agreement that would have me changing the future of Kurzak for good or bad if we were successful. Wiping out slavery would clearly be good, but I couldn't even think about what would happen if we killed all of the lords. What about their families and friends? Would I be making new enemies for Faermont and myself by my actions?

"You seem deep in thought Wess, what concerns you?" Samantha asked.

I laughed then responded, "You mean besides the fact that we are about to walk into a dungeon designed by a demon who has dreamed up creative ways to kill us?"

She didn't respond; I guess after a few hundred years I would get good at reading people too. She knew that there was something more. "I was thinking about just how large of an impact my decisions are having now. I feel like I could accidentally change the world and maybe not for the better," I said.

"I see," she said, "but don't you understand that may be exactly why you have been given these powers Wess?"

I looked over at her, the confusion clear on my face.

She continued, trying to explain, "We elves believe everything happens for a reason. Pivotal players like you are introduced when the gods have decided to change the game, for better or worse."

"Oh great," I said, "that makes me feel better; knowing I am a pawn in some big chess game of the gods."

She laughed and said, "Well who knows, maybe you are the knight or the bishop. I certainly am the queen since I can move anywhere."

We had entered into the outskirts of Answar now and I noticed a shop offering provisions. It was called, "Dungeon Delvers." It had a wooden sign with a man carrying a large sack and a pickaxe.

We stopped and stared at the store. I looked at the window and asked, "Do you have any money?"

She looked at me, and I at her, both of us knowing we had an issue without speaking it.

"Let me try something," I said

We walked to the alley next to the building and I reached out with my gift. I sent my probe down into the ground, the same way that Melikin had done with Myka's back. I felt minerals deep underground, so I asked the earth around them to help me. I closed my eyes and put my hands on the ground and pulled with my will. A small chunk of mineral worked its way up slowly at first, then picked up speed the closer it got to me. The ground spit up a green, rough rock the size of my fist.

Samantha let out a low whistle of appreciation and scooped up the rock quickly. "Probably shouldn't let anyone see that," she whispered.

I looked around. With the encroaching darkness, I didn't think anyone had seen it. "What is it?" I asked.

She dropped it into her pouch and said, "It is an emerald, can you split it? I believe we could buy the entire shop here in its current form."

My eyes went wide, "Huh, well I guess I don't need to worry about money anymore. Let me try."

She opened the pouch, and I reached out with my gift. I could feel the structure of the gem. I reached in with the earth element, spread my fingers, visualizing the flows prying at the tiny cracks. The stone shattered violently and suddenly Samantha's purse was full of tiny emerald shards.

"Well, that is almost as handy as being able to look through a frog's eyes," she said, "let's go in."

We went back to the front of the store and entered quickly. A little bell rung as we entered and an older man came out from the back and stood behind the counter. "Well, what do we have here? Two more slayers for the dungeon?"

Samantha answered, "Yes, we've come to buy some lanterns."

"Ho, ho," he laughed, "two lanterns is it? You will need more than that if you wish to survive down there! Might I be so bold as to make some recommendations?"

I looked around the shop, confused about what half of the items were. Samantha and I both nodded at the same time.

"Well, would you mind if I asked a delicate question first? It might change what I show you considerably if I knew approximately how much coin you have to spend?"

Samantha stepped forward to the counter and dumped her pouch out on it. The shop owner's eyes went wide as he stared at the green pile. Samantha spoke, breaking him out of it, "We would have anything that can help us in the dungeon."

The shop keeper looked up finally and said, "I could retire twice on this."

"I would have it so because you shall be selling no more trinkets to adventurers once we slay the demon below," Samantha said.

He nodded slowly, "Fair enough, maybe I would sleep better if one of you came back one day," he said. "Young man, would you flip that sign on the door to closed, please?"

I did as he asked. He reached under the counter and unlocked a box. Once he had it open, he pulled out a small back pack and placed it on the counter. "This is what you need," he said.

I walked to the counter with my eyebrows furrowed. The shopkeeper saw my face and held up his hand to stall my questions. "This is a magical pack. See this pocket here?" He opened the pocket and pulled out a small shiny metal rod. "Push this button once." He pushed it and the rod snapped out to a ten foot length, shooting between Samantha and me.

"It's all fun and games until someone pokes their eye out," I said dryly.

He smiled, "This rod is titanium and can apply tremendous force. Press this button and," he pressed it and short rods snapped out, staggered along its length, spaced for climbing. He pressed the top button again and the entire thing snapped back to its original form.

Samantha and I looked at each other, impressed.

"But wait! There's more," he said. "You also get this!" He opened a flap on the other side of the pack and pulled out a gold colored tube that had a lid on each side. He unscrewed one side and a beam of light shot out at the roof when he removed the lid. The light was like nothing I had ever seen. It was pure white and unwavering. He pointed it around the shop and the light was bright enough to read by within the circle it cast, but didn't spread at all.

"That is amazing," I said waving my hand through the light. I was surprised when I found that it gave no heat.

"Yes, this is considerably better than a lantern, but it gets better." He unscrewed the bottom cap and removed the tube from the lid. The light spilled everywhere and filled every corner of the room. There was a pebble mounted on the lid, and that appeared to be what was casting the light.

"How does it work?" Samantha asked.

He shrugged and said, "I have no idea, the pebble was recovered from the dungeon and sold to me years ago. I simply mounted it in the tube as I believed that would make it much more functional. I call it the light in a tube!"

We both nodded, and he continued, holding up a small vial. He said, "This will provide liquids endlessly, do not lose the lid." Then he added, "The longer it is off the faster it flows. Say the name of the liquid then remove the lid. I have used it for oil, water and even acid." He placed the vial back in the pocket.

"Well, that should come in handy," I said.

He nodded and said, "Yes, assuming you live long enough to get thirsty."

"Well, aren't you just a ray of sunshine," I said while frowning.

He snapped his fingers at me and said, "That's what I should have named my light in a tube!"

He seemed very pleased with himself, but Samantha made a frustrated hand gesture at him to indicate that he should continue. He reached into the front of the pack and pulled out an arrow. He laid it on the counter and spun it. It twirled around normally for a few seconds and then abruptly stood on its point at a slight angle toward the door.

He spoke in a hushed tone, "It is enchanted to point toward the demon below. I would advise you always go the other way, but something tells me that you two aren't going to listen. That is all the magical items that I have salvaged in the last forty three years of owning this shop with the exception of the backpack itself." He put the arrow back and opened the large flap. "The middle compartment is magical, and can call forth by name any item you put in it. I have put one of every item in this shop in this bag." He placed his arm in the pack and said, "Rope," and pulled out a coil of thick well-made rope.

He looked at us with his eyebrows raised and he could tell that we were both impressed. He put the rope back and added, "There is a list inside of every item. If you find yourself stuck inside the dungeon I would recommend you read it. I put a lot of stuff in there, so maybe something will be helpful."

He slid the pack over to us and said, "I wish you well, but I have seen many a fully armored knight and companies of adventurers go in that place, never to return. I recommend you get a room for the night and enjoy a satisfying meal. Maybe you will change your mind by morning. If you do, I would be happy to refund your gems here."

Samantha took the pack and slung it over one shoulder and said, "Our path is set, thank you for your concern." She turned and strode for the door.

I said, "Thank you sir, you have been very helpful."

As I started to leave myself, he said, "Son, just one more thing. Whatever you see down there, you should always assume it isn't safe, no matter how it appears."

He walked from behind the counter as Samantha held the door. He pointed to his leg with both hands, and I could see his right leg was a peg of wood. "I was young and foolish once, I decided to go into the dungeon to seek my fortune. Inside the first door, I stepped on a solid stone floor and fell through what was actually a painting of a floor on thin parchment. When I fell through it, I found that my leg was in the mouth of a giant armored worm that I couldn't wound with my broadsword." He got a faraway look as he told the rest, "The creature was eating my foot, and I couldn't even scratch it. I had to hack off my own leg to escape."

The next morning, Samantha and I started into the sewer. We had decided to take the man's advice as we didn't know when we would get a bed or a meal again. We stuffed a bunch of food into the pack after eating breakfast, just in case we were in the dungeon for a few days.

Everyone in the inn had a story to tell about someone they knew that didn't come back. It sounded like all types had tried it. Some, like the shopkeeper, came back, but none the richer for the experience. No one had seen the demon and lived to tell about it.

Samantha had shown me the maps so I knew what we were doing. The ruins were on a hill overlooking Answar, and there was a branch of the sewer that had served as a drain for the keep. We were not far in when we found it. Very solid looking steel bars blocked the side tunnel.

I studied the bars and the lock. I was about to try my powers on them when Samantha touched my shoulder. I looked back at her, and she leaned in with the light tube and pointed through the bars. I looked where she was pointing and saw a thin black wire running along a cross bar. I followed it with my eyes and traced it back to a tiny steel eyelet in the wall. The wire ran up the wall to the ceiling. Samantha followed it with the beam and it stopped at a release to a spiked ball on a chain in a recess in the ceiling. If we had opened the gate, it would have pulled the wire and released the spiked ball to swing down toward us.

"Well," I said, "It looks like the dungeon starts here."

I reached out with Azurain to cut through the wire so I could open the door without releasing the ball. As soon as my axe blade parted the wire, a jolt of lightning shot up my arm. My teeth clenched together and my arm muscles all seized. Everything clenched as the shock continued to pulse up my arm. I couldn't breathe, think or move, and I thought my teeth were about to shatter.

Samantha grabbed me and tried to pull me off the bars, but she seized up immediately, the shock passing to her through my body. It felt like forever, but finally Samantha blinked us forward into the hall behind the gate.

At first, my mind didn't register what was happening. We were suspended in mid-air, stuck inside some kind of clear jelly. My eyes were open and they were the first thing to start burning. It felt like the jelly was eating me everywhere.

We blinked forward again and both of us fell to the ground. I clutched at my eyes and tried to wipe the jelly from them. I got a lot off, but I was burning everywhere and my vision was blurring. It felt like it was eating my skin. Samantha rolled on the ground, trying to get the jelly off and I could see that I was not wrong, her skin on her face was bright red like it was cooked with boiling water. I knew if we didn't act quickly we were going to be in trouble.

Grabbing the pack on Samantha's back I yanked open the side pocket and pulled the magic vial out. I popped the top off and through gritted teeth I said, "Water!"

The water started trickling out. I laid on my back and poured it into my eyes and felt some relief immediately. I connected to the earth energies and flowed regenerative energy into my ruined eyes. The pain became bearable and my vision cleared. I went to Samantha and did the same for her, begging her to hold still. The water was flowing faster now and I began washing and healing her face and neck. I did my face and neck next then turned the vial back to Samantha. We both stood and used the vial to wash all the slime off next. The vial was flowing with some force now and it made clean up easier. I recapped it once we were both thoroughly clean of the goo.

I saw Samantha making a distressed face. She was trying to pull her hair back and as she pulled her hair came out in her hands. I poured a little more regenerative energy into her scalp and it grew back quickly. She hugged me fiercely. "Thank you Wess, I thought that we were both going to be digested, but even worse, I thought I would lose all my hair!"

I laughed a little and said, "We got shocked and almost digested, and you are worried about your hair." I shook my head and turned back to examine the jelly thing we had escaped.

I stepped forward and looked with my eyes and my gift. It was a living thing that was perfectly clear. I looked closer and could see a rat's skeleton in the bottom left corner still being digested. The cube had grown to fill the entire hall and apparently consumed live creatures that walked, or in our case, blinked into it.

Samantha stepped up next to me and said, "I have seen these before, but much smaller, they are used in sewers to clean the walls. Large ones normally grow to the size of my fist. This one is so large it can't even move."

I reached into the main compartment of the pack and said "Chalk."

Samantha looked at me with raised eyebrows, and as I marked the location of the creature I said, "We may be running when we return this way. It was bad enough to be digested once, I really don't want to do that again!" Once I finished, I put the chalk and the water vial back in their places.

I closed the flaps, and Samantha faced me saying, "We have been in this dungeon for about three minutes and have experienced two traps that would have killed someone without our gifts."

I looked around and shrugged, "Yeah, I am not sure if that makes me feel good or nervous. I am so good at healing that I can be stupid and still survive."

She smiled a little and said, "We just have to think like a demon; nothing will be as it appears, *ever!*"

"You're right," I said.

Samantha turned and pointed the light tube down the hall. As she did, I pulled open another pocket on her pack and pulled out the magic pole. I pushed the button to extend it to ten feet and tapped it on the ground ahead of us while we walked. I figured that it would hit any wires and trigger any traps laid in the hallway.

I was feeling pretty clever when about a hundred steps later the tapping sound of the metal pole onto stone changed its sound distinctly. It went from ting, ting, ting to thwap.

Samantha and I stopped and crouched to check the floor. Upon close inspection, we could see that painted canvas replaced the entire floor. I took Azurain and sliced the fake floor from wall to wall. When I did, it fell away from us and revealed a nasty looking pit below. There was a jumble of long sharp spikes below pointed at us. When Samantha pointed her light into the pit, we could see several skeletons in various positions around the spikes.

We stood up, and I said, "A nasty pit, but I think we can easily jump it now." I took a few steps back and was preparing to leap across.

"Wait!" Samantha yelled. "Think like a demon Wess."

I stared at her considering then nodded. I walked back to the pit and studied it a bit longer. Out loud I asked myself, "What would I do if I were a demon?"

Samantha answered for me, "Maybe I would place another trap on the floor where someone would land if they did jump over."

I looked at her and nodded, "Yeah that does seem like something a demon might do. Maybe you have a little demon blood in you, Samantha!" She glared at me, and I shrugged and added, "Maybe all girls have a little demon blood in them."

I reached across with the ten foot pole and tapped along the far side of the pit. I felt no wires, and nothing exploded. I walked back and forth and tapped the entire floor, even pressing down in case there was a trap requiring some weight to trigger. I pulled the pole back and said, "The floor seems clear, but I will armor myself in stone just in case."

"We could just blink across," she said.

"We saw what that can get us, though," I replied.

I snapped the pole back to its compact size and backed up to get a running start. I decided I would add the stone after I jumped as I can run faster without it. I ran three steps, leapt into the air and armored myself. I sailed through the air and saw that I was going to easily clear the pit and land on the other side. Just before I did, I struck something at chest height. It felt like a thin wire pulled across my chest. My foot was inches from the other side, and I was thrown backwards down into the pit.

My rock armor shattered the spikes and bones as I crashed down into the pit. I found myself lying in the bottom looking up at Samantha, the spikes I didn't crush on my way down forming an outline of my rock form.

Samantha covered her mouth and giggled at me. I sighed and stood up, dropping my rock armor as I did. I pushed the top and middle button on the pole and it extended and popped out its climbing rungs. I leaned it against the other side and climbed from the pit, pulling the pole up and retracting the climbing rungs.

Samantha blinked across and said, "I know we made that shop keeper rich, but I feel like we should tip him if we make it out of this."

My response was interrupted by the sound of something that sounded like a stone ball rolling toward us. Samantha swiveled the light, and we saw that it was exactly what it sounded like. A ball taller than me, made of stone, was rolling at us very quickly. It would crush us both in a matter of seconds.

I tried to remain calm and reached out with my gift and felt it for any cracks. I spread my fingers and right before the ball rolled over us, I cracked it in half. The top half of the ball split off and slid to a stop right in front of us. The piece in back flipped over halfway on top of it.

I looked at Samantha and said, "This demon was thorough in his trap building. Had we found the wire and climbed across we would have likely leapt back into the pit to avoid the ball. He could have actually killed three people with this."

Samantha and I stared at the traps for a while before we climbed over and continued down the hall.

Within about one hundred careful steps, we found stone rails that went at an angle into the ceiling. We could see a large rounded opening where the ball was released from.

I looked at Samantha and said, "Maybe I should walk ahead armored from now on."

"Seems like a sound plan," she said.

I layered myself in rock and took the flashlight in one hand and the pole in the other. Azurain rested on my belt, and I wished I had a third hand. I thought that it would be really cool if I could just strap the light tube to my forehead.

I walked about fifteen steps and the pole hit a wire. I heard a twang, and a snap, then a beam flipped up from the floor in front of me, launching darts in my direction. My instinct was to dodge, but instead I raised both my hands above me, so none of the darts would make it past. "Tink, tink, tink, tink, tink." The darts bounced off my rock armor and fell harmlessly to the hall in front of me.

I looked back with the light and Samantha gave a thumbs up sign. I continued on gaining confidence in my plan. I triggered another trap just five steps later as a floor plate shifted under me. I laughed as a block of stone dropped from the ceiling and shattered on my rock skull. I walked on unscathed.

I pointed the light ahead and could see a large solid looking door at the end of the hallway. Just before I arrived at it, a long razor blade swung toward me from the wall and smashed into my waist. It didn't penetrate my armor, but the force was so strong that it pinched me against the wall. I had to slide out sideways from behind the blade.

Samantha laughed and said, "I guess you don't need to think like a demon, if you can walk like a boulder."

I looked back at her and said, "Yeah, this is way better than thinking!"

I grabbed the handle of the door and turned the latch. Instead of opening on hinges on the side like all doors do, I heard the latch release in the top of the door. I looked up, confused, as the spring loaded door pivoted from the bottom and flattened me to the floor. The spring was so strong I could barely breathe. Spikes had also erupted from the door, but had failed to penetrate my rock form.

There was a blur of movement above me, and I grunted as Samantha planted her foot on the door and sprang into the room.

The sounds of battle rang out inside the room, I laid there confused and stuck.

Chapter 16: Sword

I needed to get into that room and help Samantha. I tried pushing against the door, but it wouldn't move at all. I examined the spikes with my gift and decided to try something creative. I bent my will to the two spikes on the sides above me and made them lengthen. Each spike grew longer and thinner, extending past me to press into the stone floor. Slowly, the door raised off my chest and I was able to pull myself free.

I leapt up on top of the door and charged into the room. Samantha was being pressed hard by four of Rissling's ogres. I pulled Azurain out as I charged in. Samantha blinked behind one ogre who was wielding a gigantic greatsword and shoved her blade into its ribs from behind. The ogre next to it pulled back a large black iron mace to crush Samantha as she tried to remove her blade. My axe took the beast in the throat and it fell dead with a confused look on its face.

The other two ogres made a huge mistake then as they swiveled to face an unarmed boy. I charged in hard and pulled my empty hand back. The ogre on the left poked out with a spear and I shrugged it aside as it bounced of my rock shoulder. I swung my right arm down and willed Azurain to me. My weapon appeared in my empty hand just in time to bury itself in the ogre's chest. The ogre let out a gurgling scream and fell on its back thrashing in pain.

I willed Azurain back to my hand, but the last ogre caught me in the side of the head with its club. Even with the rock armor my ears rang and I fell on my side from the powerful blow.

Samantha suddenly appeared on it shoulders with both blades held high. She plunged them downward right through the creature's collar bones and into its chest. As I stood, it dropped to its knees then fell flat on its face. Samantha stepped off of it in front of me and said, "While you were playing with the door you missed saying hello to your friend Rissling."

"He was here?" I asked, looking around. Now that I had a chance to really study the room I could see dead ogres everywhere. There were also strange blue piles of goo near many of them. I counted twenty-four dead ogres lying about the room. The room was large and square and had debris on the floor from stone columns that had been destroyed. Part of the roof had collapsed, and there was a hallway to our left with stairs heading up, and a hallway to the right with stairs going down.

I looked back to Samantha and asked, "Did you kill all these ogres? I wasn't under that door that long was I?"

She said, "Yes he was here, and no I didn't kill all of them. When I came in Rissling was there," she pointed at a wall of alcoves at the back of the room, "looking at that alcove. I blinked straight to him after I killed an ogre, but he used his ring to teleport out. I only killed six ogres, the rest were dead when I came in."

I dropped the rock armor, handed Samantha the light, and walked over to the alcoves she had pointed to. I saw a jade figurine of a unicorn in the middle alcove. It was expertly carved and the moment I saw it I thought of Myka. I picked it up and studied it. Samantha came to stand by me, and I dropped it in my pouch. I turned to face her and she just stood there looking at me with raised eyebrows.

"I thought this might help with my friend Myka," I said. "She is going to be angry at me when I get home. I can imagine explaining to her why I left without saying goodbye and ended up traveling the world with a beautiful elven princess, warrior-chick." I frowned, "Yeah, she is going to kill me."

Samantha smiled and said, "You think I'm beautiful?"

I blushed and stammered, "Well, I mean uh, sure, I guess."

I paused and took a deep breath, "You are easily the prettiest ogre slayer I have ever met."

Smiling, she tussled my hair, "You are pretty cute yourself, when you aren't in rock form anyway. If I wasn't four hundred years older than you I am sure I would find you quite charming."

That really didn't help my blushing and I found I couldn't meet her gaze. She laughed again and turned toward the stairs.

Great, I thought, I am "cute". I really wanted to be handsome or something, but not cute. Cute was for kids and puppies.

Samantha walked to the top of the stairs and pointed the light down them. As I walked up next to her, I could see that the stairs went down sharply and curved to the left. They were pretty wide at the top, where we were standing, but narrowed before the turn.

Samantha took a single step and the stairs suddenly flattened into a ramp. Her feet shot out from under her and oil squirted from holes in the walls. Before I could react, she flew down the ramp and followed the bend in the hall. I leapt after her and changed into owl form, chasing the rapidly receding light.

I flew as fast as I could after her, but the hallway steadily curved to the left and the ramp had her moving faster than I could go. I could see the light ahead, but it was getting dimmer by the second.

I flapped my wings hard and maintained the constant bank. Suddenly, the light ahead flickered wildly then disappeared for a moment. I kept flying, my owl eyes serving me well. Finally I came to the end of the ramp; it emptied near the roof of a huge cavern. I burst into the cavern and tucked my wings as I saw the light well below me tumbling into the darkness.

I heard a splash from below and the light started refracting from the water, bouncing off the walls of the cavern. With the light bouncing, I could see we were in a giant underground cavern filled with water. On the other side of the cavern, was a ledge and a hallway that continued on. I took all of this in as I was diving straight toward my friend.

She surfaced then, but the light was still spinning below her and I was sure she had dropped it in the water. As the light spun through the water, I saw a huge dark shape swim under her. The light spun the right way, and I could see clearly that it was a giant white shark.

The creature turned under Samantha, swimming straight up for her with its massive jaws opened. I shrieked a warning, my wings still tucked, diving straight for her. She was treading water, looking around confused. She clearly had no sense of her doom.

I was forced to pull up as the shark exploded from the water, clamping its massive jaws on Samantha's body. Blood exploded from her, and I was sure I was about to see my friend bit in half. She flailed around in pain her head twisting back and forth. The shark hung in the air for a second with Samantha in its mouth then started to fall back toward the water. I watched in horror and could think of nothing I could do to help. The shark bit down as it fell back to the water and Samantha was just suddenly gone. I looked around frantically and saw her lying on the ledge bleeding from a dozen places. I flapped my wings, pulling hard toward the ledge and began flooding healing energy into her. I was relieved to feel that she still held a strong spark of life.

I landed and released the owl form, quickly placing my hands on her wounds. I closed them all with a thought and healed her crushed ribs and punctured lung. Her breathing became steady and I sat cross legged, pulling her head onto my lap. I flowed more regenerative energy into her, and before long her eyes fluttered open.

"Well that hurt," she said.

I couldn't help but chuckle a little. "That is why you let boulder boy go first," I said.

I looked down the hall, but couldn't see much without the light. Samantha tried to stand and I helped her up. She reached down to her swords, and I saw her shoulders slump visibly. I looked down to see that one of her swords was missing and the other one was bent in the middle. I reached down and yanked a shark tooth out of the side of her sheath where the sword had crumpled.

"That sword probably saved your life," I said, handing her the tooth.

She sighed, "That's all well and good, but without a usable weapon, I might as well be dead down here."

I replied, "Maybe I can find it when I go get the light."

She unbuckled her bent sword and leaned it against the wall, nodding. "I guess I will wait here." She pulled the pack off, said, "knife," and pulled out a large, wicked looking dagger. She placed it on her hip and started ringing out her hair. I found myself observing her ripped clothing from where the shark had bit her and decided I better go before she noticed me ogling her. She might be four hundred, but she looked twenty. I shook myself and turned away, trying to keep my mind focused.

I took two steps toward the ledge and dove out toward the water. I hit it quickly and pulled in a large air bubble around my head with my gift. I had the water propel me down toward the light quickly and before I knew it I was on the bottom. The shark swam by me several times, but paid me no attention. I was ready to have the water shoot him up in the air if he got too close, but like all natural animals, this one seemed to like me. I wasn't angry at it for trying to eat my friend. It was just a shark doing what sharks do.

I scooped up the light tube and looked around for Samantha's sword. I didn't see it, so I reached out with my gift and tied to sense any metal. I was surprised to sense a lot of metal beneath me. This wasn't a chunk of mineral. I could feel that this was many pieces of armor. I pulled it all up with my gift, the sand parting easily for me.

Soon a skeletal knight greeted me with a dead man's smile. The knight was wearing a full suit of armor, minus the helmet, and a sword on his belt. I imagined that he had slid down the same stair ramp we had and sunk like a rock. There were no bite marks on his armor and it looked well preserved. I didn't think either Samantha or I could fit it, so I unbuckled the sword and swam back to the surface. Just to show off, I had the water lift me back to the ledge, and I stepped off of the spout like some kind of water spirit. I probably ruined it with my cheesy grin, but Samantha only had eyes for the sword.

I handed it to her and pointed the light down the tunnel. As she inspected the weapon, I stood there and scanned for traps. It was a natural stone tunnel with a rough ceiling and walls. I didn't see any, so I assumed that meant I was about to get blown up with my first step.

I looked back to Samantha as she pulled the blade from its sheath. Once the sword was clear from its home a blue flame lit along the entire blade. I covered the light tube with my hand and was pleased to see that the sword was casting its own strong steady light.

Samantha placed her hand over the flame and looked up at me, confused. "The flame is cool to the touch," she said.

I put my hand near the flame and yanked it back quickly as my flesh started cooking. "That wasn't funny," I muttered.

"It burned you?" she asked, sounding confused. She stared at the sword for a moment then said, "I wonder if that means I am immune to all fire or just this sword's heat."

"Hmm, I think we may want to find that out," I said. I walked to the pack and said, "Torch."

I pulled out the oil soaked torch and waived it above the flaming sword. It burst into a healthy red flame immediately, and I held it out for Samantha. With the sword in one hand she placed her other hand near the flame for a moment, then thrust it inside the flame and smiled at me.

"Well, maybe that shark bite was worth it after all," I said. "I think that is going to be an awesome party trick."

She pulled her hand out of the flame then sheathed her sword, the light dimming considerably when she did. She kept her hand on the hilt then felt the flame again. Lastly, she removed her hand and just let it hang from her hip. Once again she reached out for the flame, but this time she pulled her hand back quickly. "The sword extends proof from fire, but I must be touching it. This is a wonderful find Wess, thank you!"

"No problem, I am just happy you are armed again."

She seemed to be done with the torch, so I tossed it in the water. I had the water bring it back to me on a spout and I grabbed it and shoved it back in the pack.

I looked back at Samantha, and she had her hands on her hips with her eyebrows raised, "Now you are just showing off."

"No, I was showing off before too." I grinned stupidly at her before I armored up. I walked past her with the light tube, prepared for something else to smash into my face.

The cave tunnel sloped down steadily and after about ten minutes of no traps I got concerned that maybe we were going the wrong way. I stopped and dropped my rock armor, waiting for Samantha to catch up.

"What's going on?" she whispered, "Did you hear something?"

"No," I replied, "That's what's bothering me. Maybe this isn't the right way."

I reached into the pack's side pocket and pulled out the magic arrow. I spun it on the ground and it stood on its point, aiming sideways and down to the hall.

"That's not very helpful," she said.

I picked it up and placed it back in the pack. "Well, at least we know he is still below us," I replied.

A realization struck me then and I thought back to escaping the arena and finding Azurain. "Hang on, let me try something."

I reached out with my gift and felt the rock around me. I had never changed into a bat before, but I felt like this is how they saw in the dark. I closed my eyes and by sensing where the stone was I got a clear sense of where it wasn't.

I focused on our level and below, since I knew we didn't want to go up. I spoke out loud as I started to visualize a map of our surroundings, "There is a large cavern a long way down this tunnel, there are many tunnels out of it, and one goes back this way, but under us. Over there," I pointed down and back the way we had come, "is a large man made room. There is one hall off of that room going to some stairs that way." I pointed in the way that the arrow had originally shown.

I opened my eyes and said, "I could open a tunnel to that room from up here and we could skip whatever is waiting for us down there." I pointed down the tunnel we had been walking.

Samantha nodded, "It seems reasonable, and I like anything that has us doing something the demon wouldn't expect. He is unlikely to build traps for places where no one would ever travel."

I nodded and began walking back the way we had come. After about twenty paces, we were about forty feet above the room I had sensed. "Be ready," I said, "I don't know what is in that room."

Samantha pulled her new flaming sword out with her right hand and held her dagger in the other. I motioned for her to stand behind me and I closed my eyes and connected to the earth energies. I bent my will to the stone and asked it to make a tunnel down to the room below us. The stone complied with my thoughts and started separating in front of me. The earth groaned and complained, but slowly the tunnel opened. I felt the walls and ceiling around me start to weaken and I had some stone shift to support it. I opened my eyes to see a ramp going down into the darkness, and I could sense the room below.

Aiming the light down the ramp, I saw two red circles reflecting back at me from the room below. I frowned, unsure at what I was seeing. I armored up and started walking down the ramp, focusing the light on the two red dots. About half way down the light started to illuminate the room, and I realized I was looking at something's eyes. The shape of a large head was visible in the room below and I thought I might be staring at a statue. We walked on and with each pace I could make out more detail. Not only was there one head facing us but there was a second head right next to it facing away from us. As we got to the lip of the ramp, I crouched to get a full look at the creature.

I was now positive it wasn't a statue as it was clearly made of flesh. The creature stood almost to the ceiling of the large stone room. I was guessing it was about fifteen feet tall. It was a strange thing made of many body parts that looked like they were crudely sewn together. It had two heads facing opposite directions and four arms. Two of the arms were attached at the shoulder, but the one on the left was facing backwards, the same direction the head on the right was. It had another huge arm that was larger than the others attached to its chest and the last was connected to its back. Its body was misshapen and not proportioned correctly, and it had a big extra section in the middle that actually had different color skin. This thing was really gross looking.

Around its neck hung a key and the only other thing in the room was a chest with a stout lock. To the right of the creature was an open hallway. The creature stood there staring at me as I examined it, not moving at all.

I reflected on my earlier thoughts about having a third hand and decided that I would never ask for extra body parts again.

"Creepy," I whispered.

I almost fell into the room when Samantha touched my shoulder. I stood and slid to the side to let her get a better view. She studied it for a moment then turned to me, asking, "What do you think is in that chest?"

"I don't know, but I am thinking we shouldn't mess with this thing if we can avoid it," I said.

"I could blink us to that hall over there."

I shook my head, "Remember what happened last time we blinked into a hall?"

"All of this feels too obvious," she said.

I nodded and put my hand to my chin and studied the room. "There are two obvious choices here. One is to try and fight the creature to gain access to the chest and the other is to simply go around it to the left and exit the hall. I think the demon wants us to do either of those, so we shouldn't. We need to find a new choice, I think."

I crouched down and looked at the creature again, "Hey, can you understand me?"

Nothing, it just stared at me.

I reached out with my gift and felt no life in the creature, its heart wasn't beating and it drew no breath. I was sure that it was being animated with some kind of dark magic. If it wasn't alive it couldn't make decisions. The magic would likely be triggered by events. If I was the demon I would have it be triggered by one of the obvious events people would take.

I sat there staring at it trying to think like a demon. My instinct was to try and destroy it, so this meant that I shouldn't do that. My second instinct was to avoid it completely, so once again I decided I should not do that either.

I spoke aloud to myself and Samantha, "The demon made this thing hideously ugly, so that we would want to destroy it or avoid it. The last thing I want to do is get near it, so I think we need to do exactly that."

I reached out with my gift and reshaped the rock above the creature opening up the ceiling and making a ledge for me to stand on. Samantha stood ready with her weapons, but I hoped she would not need them. I walked to the ledge, standing directly over the abomination. I knelt and bent over the creature's heads. As I did, it tilted both its heads back and stared at me. I almost threw up when I saw that the second head had two faces stitched together. I had to work hard to keep my breathing steady. The chain holding the key was looped around both of its necks.

I put my left hand on the ledge and with my right I leaned slowly down and carefully took the chain from the creature's shoulder. It was difficult to do as my hand was shaking. I lifted it slowly up and over its left head and then the right. The creature didn't move at all as I did this and I was glad to be free of it, quickly standing.

I walked back to Samantha and she said, "Well done Wess, I didn't want to say anything, but I was pretty sure if we attacked the creature we would have ended up its next body part addition."

"Eww, that's so gross," I replied. "Do we open the chest now?"

Samantha shook her head, "Once again that feels like the obvious thing to do to me. I think we hold onto the key and go down that hall, maybe we will need it."

I nodded in agreement, slid the key off the chain and dropped it in my pouch. Without another word, Samantha sheathed her dagger and blinked us down into the room. We both clutched our weapons, ready as we side-stepped to the hall, but the creature just kept staring at us. Finally, we turned and stepped into the hall. I took a full breath and relaxed a little, glad to be out of the room.

Samantha and I walked about four steps into the hall and two glass walls dropped from the ceiling. One in front of me and another behind her, trapping us in a small room. Holes appeared vertically, all along the walls to our left and right. I spun, trying to figure out what was happening.

Water began shooting out of the holes and filling the small space we were in. Samantha grabbed my shoulder, but nothing happened. She looked surprised when she said, "I can't use my powers."

I tried connecting to the earth to plug the holes and found myself shielded, unable to feel the flows at all. I looked down and realized I was no longer armored in rock. Something was killing our magic here. The water was up to our ankles now, and I was starting to panic. This hallway was as tall as the room, but it was going to fill very quickly at this rate.

"I can't use my gift either, but maybe I can break the glass," I said. I pulled Azurain from my belt and slammed it into the glass as hard as I could. It bounced off hard and jarred my elbow and shoulder in the process. My hand opened from the pain and Azurain dropped into the water. I willed it back to my hand and nothing happened. The water was up to my knees as I bent to collect my axe. Now I was seriously freaking out.

Samantha started searching all along the walls, pushing and pulling on each of the stones. I started doing the same on the other wall, trying to focus on something other than drowning in this little room.

"I don't understand," I said, "I feel like we did everything right back there."

Samantha responded, "Maybe we were supposed to open the chest. Maybe there was something in there we needed to get out of this room. Maybe there wasn't a right answer, maybe this entire place is just meant to kill us all no matter what!"

My hands kept working up the rows of stone, all of them felt tight. "I have been thinking about that. The demon has been bound here for a thousand years and he has like four hundred left to go right?"

"Yes, that's right." She said.

The water was up to my chest now. I could smell the salt, and I imagined it was coming from the large area above us with the shark.

"All right, so the demon is required to protect the artifact by contract. So, what happens if someone gets through and gets the artifact? Is he released back to his realm? Does he face some sort of punishment? I mean, there must be a reason that the traps are devious, but have a solution if you are clever. I mean, why even build a dungeon? Why not collapse the entire place and bury it?

Why even make it possible? I think Jerzatu wants someone to get through, but he needs to make sure whoever does get through is smart enough to accomplish something he wants done. Maybe he wants someone smart enough to figure out how to free him from this realm."

I was swimming now, bouncing on my toes to keep my head above water. I looked over at Samantha and she had given up feeling the rocks too.

"These are all wonderful thoughts Wess, but apparently we weren't smart enough to make it through. So, if you are right in your thinking it just means we weren't the ones, even with Crimsura and Azurain." Samantha said the last part with a sad tone and I could tell she was starting to accept that we were going to die here.

It made me angry, there was something we were missing. The obvious choice here again was to blame ourselves and drown. I wasn't ready to do that. The water was a foot from the ceiling now and still filling fast.

"Samantha, this room is water tight right?" I asked.

She nodded, "It certainly appears to be!"

"So, where is the air going?" I asked.

She looked at me with eyes wide and we both looked up at the same time. Right above me was a large key hole. I held my breath and grabbed my pouch with both hands, sinking under the water as I did. I jammed my right hand inside and stabbed myself on the little unicorn figurine. I yanked my hand back instinctively and the bag turned inside out, dumping the key and the unicorn.

I popped up above the water and shouted, "I dropped the key!"

There was about six inches left and Samantha was on her back so she could breathe. She turned her head, gulped in a breath and dove down. I did the same trying not to panic and failing. My heart was racing and my chest was seizing up. I dove with my eyes open, pushing off from the ceiling with my feet. The salt water was greenish in color and I didn't even see the bottom until I crashed into it.

My hands franticly searched the stone and I bumped into Samantha several times. I was having to kick my feet hard to remain on the bottom, so I let some air out. It helped immediately and I was rewarded when I felt something on the ground. I patted it with my hand and realized it was the figurine. I snatched it, but was out of air.

I pushed off the bottom and put both hands above me to feel for the ceiling. I let the air out of my lungs and prepared to take a breath before diving again. My hands crashed into the ceiling without breaking free of the water and I realized I was as good as dead. There was no air left.

I tried to pivot and push off again, but I didn't even have the strength. My heart was beating in my head, and my body was screaming for air. I knew not to take a breath, but it didn't matter anymore, I couldn't resist the urge. I opened my mouth and sucked in a huge lungful of water as I sank slowly toward the bottom. My vision blurred and I could feel my heart pounding slower than it should be.

Chapter 18: Blob-a-pedes

My vision was blurring, my mind floating away and suddenly I was pulled by the water, falling quickly then tumbling on the floor. I felt hands on my chest, but I was still floating. Lips, I felt lips. They were soft and warm I floated into them. I felt a sting on my face once, then again. My eyes flew open and water heaved from my lungs. Samantha rolled me on my side. I tried to breathe and get the water out at the same time. I choked, gagged, then sneezed, and threw up salt water. My lungs felt like they were on fire as I breathed in my first full breath.

I rolled onto my back, clutched Azurain, and tried to connect to the flows. Even in my condition I connected quickly this time and immediately healed my lungs. The relief to my chest was instant and my head stopped throbbing as the regenerative power of the earth did its work. I looked at Samantha leaning on the wall opposite from me. She was soaked through with her hair smashed to her forehead. She had never looked more beautiful to me.

"Did you kiss me?" I asked.

She snorted a laugh and pushed her hair back, "You wish! I was breathing for you. You know, so you wouldn't die?"

"Soooo, you did put your lips on mine though, right? I am going to count that as a kiss. Don't worry, I would do the same for you any time!" I laughed at my own humor, I thought I was being down right adorable.

She shook her head and mutterd, "*Usen-linga!*" She stood and picked up her flaming sword, raising it to examine the hall.

I was pretty sure I didn't want to know what Usen-linga meant so, I decided that it meant awesome-dude. I stood then and dropped the unicorn figurine back into my pouch. I was surprised that I had managed to hold onto it, even when I had almost drowned. Somehow, I didn't think Myka was going to fully appreciate my efforts to bring her this trinket.

I walked to Samantha's side, and she handed me the light tube. "You are in the lead lover boy," she said.

I quickly pulled on my rock armor to hide my blushing. I stepped forward and took the lead with the light. I suddenly realized that I didn't have the pole. I had to think back, the last place I remembered having it was when I was flattened by the door. I was sure it was still laying up there on the floor.

I was cursing myself for forgetting it when I stepped on a circular stone. There was a click and a blast of super cold frost shot up from the floor and down from the roof. I was instantly frozen in place, and within a few seconds was completely encased in an ice shell.

The blast of white shut off and through the ice, I could see something moving toward us. It was low to the ground, but the ice was blurring my vision and refracting the light, making it tough to make out. It looked like a big white snake slithering along the floor by the wall. I decided I didn't want to wait and see if it was friendly.

I pulled in energy from the earth and shifted my form to that of a large grizzly bear. The ice exploded off of me and I shook my fur, removing the small pieces clinging there.

Now I could see the creature clearly, and I wasn't sure if it was a natural animal or not. I shifted back to my form as Samantha arrived next to me. We studied the creature together. It had a white sectional blobby body, being propelled by hundreds of legs. It was about twenty feet long and had two antennae on top of its head. It was moving very slowly in a snake like pattern and had a round mouth that pulsed in a gross kind of way. It was moving about as slow as if I walked backwards, but I had the strange feeling that I did not want to get caught by it.

I decided to check and see if I could command it like I could with most natural animals. I held out my hand and said, "Stop!"

Not surprisingly, the white, blobby, giant centipede thing didn't stop. I put my rock armor on and ran up next to it. I lifted Azurain, and it slowly started to turn in my direction. My blade lengthened and thinned as I chopped down on it. I easily severed the creature neatly in half. Instead of dying, the front half kept turning toward me with its silly little mouth.

It surprised me then when the back half sprouted a new mouth and two antenna. I took several quick steps back as the new mouth started making kissy faces at me too. This thing was seriously creepy!

I heard Samantha say, "Oil!" Suddenly she was there pouring oil all along the thing's back. I kept backing up and they kept creeping toward me.

Samantha took her time and covered every inch of the creature. Once it was soaked in the black goo, she aimed it at the next one. It was flowing well now and the little white wormy thing was covered quickly. She ran past them both, holding the vial so that it covered the floor behind her. When she arrived at my side she covered the vial again and unsheathed her sword. The blue flames sprang to life even before the blade was all the way free of the scabbard.

She turned and touched the oil with her sword, watching as it erupted into flame and charged toward the worms. The giant white worms were engulfed immediately, but they did not change their course at all. Samantha unstopped the vial and commanded oil again. We stood there and sprayed them down with oil until they burned to nothing. The smell of burning lumpy worm was quite disgusting and we were forced to take a few steps back.

I looked at Samantha and said, "I don't know about you, but I am kind of hungry."

She made a face at me that said, "Eww."

I laughed and decided I would wait to eat until we got to fresher air, but I really was hungry. I shrugged and turned to continue down the hall. There were three more of the giant centipede things silently creeping up behind us. They didn't make a sound and they were almost close enough to touch. Two of them were on the ground, but the third was walking sideways on the wall.

I grabbed Samantha's hand and ran down the middle of the hall, pulling her along behind me. Once I got past them I hugged the wall and continued moving up the hall. I figured if they had just come from this way maybe the edges of the hall would be free of traps.

We burst into a spacious natural stone cavern and I slammed to a halt, my eyes going wide. The cavern was full of the gross blob-a-pedes. They were all turning and slowly crawling toward us. Some dropped from the ceiling, others winded down stalactites. They were everywhere, and there were hundreds of them.

"We have to keep going." Samantha said urgently.

The closest worms were about six feet from us. I said, "Let's wait as long as we can and draw them to us, then you can blink us past them."

We backed up a little more, and I checked over my shoulder to make sure the other ones weren't going to start sucking on the back of my leg or something. They were still about eight feet away, so I focused instead on finding a spot we could blink to.

I scanned around the room with the light. I saw several open spots, but the worms were clearly avoiding these areas. It made me think that there was a reason and not random. The spots they were avoiding were all the same size.

"I think those spots are traps!" I said.

Samantha nodded and said, "That doesn't leave us a lot of room to work!"

She grabbed my shoulder, and we blinked forward. We appeared, standing on top of two worms. I landed off center on my worm and I started falling away from Samantha. Instinctively, I leapt away before I fell and shifted into an owl, flapping hard to gain some height from the worms.

Samantha blinked forward two more times, each time landing on the back of one of the white worms. I flew hard trying to catch up, and one of the creatures dropped from the ceiling narrowly missing me. I looked down to see the entire cavern of worms turning toward Samantha as she ported to the exit. I landed next to her and dropped my owl form.

"Come into the hall and I will shape the stone closed behind us," I said.

She nodded and I took one step into the hall. The floor exploded under me in a wave of force. I am not sure if the whomp noise was in my head or from the explosion, but both my ears exploded in pain as I flew through the air head over heels.

I landed hard on the worms and bounced off several of them. I screamed in pain as mouths latched onto me in several places. I felt them sucking my life and strength from me. My head was ringing, the room spinning and I was having trouble thinking.

I thought back to the lesson Samantha had given me about controlling myself when I needed to. I focused all my will on connecting to the earth and ignored the worms crawling on top of me to find a free place to attach their mouths. It took all my will power to draw a tiny trickle, but it was enough to armor myself in rock. I felt better instantly, the worms could no longer pull my life energy through my skin. I started pulling energy in to heal myself and as I did I felt my connection to the earth strengthen.

I stood, pushing off on the worms and looked for Samantha. I couldn't see her, but my heart dropped into my stomach when I saw a pile of worms twisting and squirming in a pile. I ran through them and jammed my hand into the bottom of the pile. I felt Samantha at the bottom and poured healing energy into her. I heard her gasp, but the worms started growing rapidly. I was feeding them by healing her.

"Samantha!" I yelled, "Blink straight up, now!"

Suddenly, I wasn't touching her anymore. I stood up and caught her as she appeared above me and fell into my arms. I poured more rock energy into me and made myself larger and thicker. I walked slowly and steadily to the exit while healing Samantha. Every inch of her had bright red pucker marks from the creature's disgusting lips. I waded through them, kicking them out of my way. I was pretty sure I was going to have nightmares about this forever.

I put Samantha down just inside the hall and summoned Azurain back to my hand. I reached my hands out, making a pulling motion toward the walls and made the rock close off on the worms. When I did, it got very dark in the hallway and I realized that I dropped the light tube somewhere back in the room when I had shifted to the owl form.

Samantha pulled her flaming sword out and I said, "Great! I left the light back in there!"

Samantha gave me a little hug and said, "Thank you, Wess. That was pretty awful in there. I owe Jerzatu for those things when we meet him. Those could have only come from the mind of a demon."

"Speaking of which," I pointed down the hall, "there is a door there with some writing above it, and it looks like a math problem!"

Chapter 19: Math

Samantha raised her sword up, and we studied the door. It wasn't far, but I wanted to make sure we weren't going to get blown up again. "Stay here a second." I said.

I plugged my ears and stomped my rock legs up to the door. Nothing happened, so I waived Samantha up and we studied it together. Twelve black metal marbles were stuck to the door randomly inside of a white circle. Chiseled above the door was a puzzle, it read:

Twelve marbles here form seven
rows of four. Turn the knob and
continue the tour. Fail at the math
and I promise a blood bath.

Jerzatu

"Great!" I said in despair, "now he is signing his name on his traps."

Samantha was staring at the words, deep in thought. I rambled on, venting my frustration, "This is stupid! Seven rows of four would not be twelve!" I crossed my arms and grumbled, "Seven rows of four would take twenty eight marbles!" I looked at Samantha shocked at myself. I was never good at math and I just did that quickly in my head.

She looked at me her eyebrows raised, "Seven rows of four would be more than twenty eight if you counted the vertical rows." She pointed at the words and said, "I think they are giving us a hint. Your instinct was to think in rows left to right, but a row is any line in any direction. We must think differently to solve this as we have had to with every trap in this place."

She took the pack off and asked for chalk. She sat cross legged on the ground and started doodling with it.

I was bored and really didn't want to think about this stupid puzzle. I wanted to punch through the door, but I was sure it would explode in my face or something. I watched Samantha drawing on the ground and couldn't stand the silence.

I spoke, "So, these artifacts enhance all of our abilities both natural and magical. I mean, it made me actually decent in a fight against you. I wonder if they actually make us smarter."

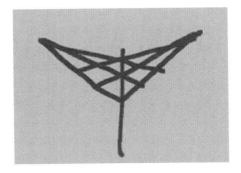

She looked up at me and said, "I think they do." She pointed at what she had drawn on the ground.

I looked down at it and said, "Huh, yeah I see it. Put a marble at each intersection and you have seven rows of four. Brilliant Samantha!"

She smiled up at me, and I turned back to the door arranging the marbles quickly. I had to look down at what Samantha had drawn a few times to get them to line up, but with the diagram it wasn't too hard.

Once I had it, I looked back to Samantha, who was now standing with her pack back on. She studied it before nodding. I grabbed the latch and turned it. The marbles lit up and the door opened easily. I sighed when I could see another door about twenty feet in, with more writing above it.

"You shouldn't have put the chalk away," I said.

I walked forward to the door, angry now that I had to do another math problem. I stomped toward the door and hit a trip wire halfway down the hall. A steel spear shot out into my chest and smashed me into the opposite wall. "Oh, come on!" I yelled.

Samantha put her hand on my shoulder, "You would have been dead Wess, if you weren't armored. Calm yourself and be cautious. You are not invulnerable."

I slid out from under the spear and took a deep breath. "You're right, sorry, I am just tired of this place," I said. We went to the door, and Samantha lifted the sword, so we could read the puzzle.

Remove five coins from the eleven,
add four coins and leave nine

In the middle of the door was a bowl and sure enough there was eleven coins in it. Samantha and I both stared into the bowl. I put my hand on my chin, for some reason I felt like that helped me think.

"OK, if we take out five," I took five out and held them in my palm. "Then we put four back in." I put four from my palm into the bowl. "That gets us ten in the bowl." I frowned, feeling like I missed something obvious.

"You are doing the obvious thing, think like a demon," Samantha said.

I put all the coins back and put my hand on my chin again, studying the words. Apparently, my chin didn't have the magical thought powers I was hoping for. I started rubbing it slowly and found myself wondering when I would grow a beard.

"We have company," Samantha whispered.

I looked over my shoulder and saw white worms crawling down the hall toward us. I sighed and turned back to the coins. "All right, there is no way to do anything different with the first part, so, I will remove five from the eleven." I muttered to myself and took five coins out and bounced them in my palm.

I looked at the puzzle again and tried to think of a different way to look at the words, *add four coins*. "I took that as adding four back to the bowl, but what if I added four more to my hand?" I said. I took four more out, now I had nine in my hand. I read the last part, *and leave nine*. I turned my palm over and dumped them on the floor. I grabbed the handle and confidently swung it open away from me.

"Maybe my chin is smart after all," I said

Thankfully, the door swung into a cavern and not another puzzle trap. We stepped inside and shut the door against the horde of sucker face worms following us.

Samantha held the sword up as high as she could, but we couldn't see the ceiling in the darkness. The cavern was massive, spreading into the darkness left, right, and in front of us. I went to the pack and pulled out the arrow again. I knelt and spun it on the floor.

I was watching it spin when Samantha dove on me and blinked us forward. We continued rolling and I heard a crash on the ground where I had been kneeling a moment before. I rolled to my knees and saw a short stalactite embedded in the stone, point down where I had been kneeling just a moment ago.

We watched in horror as it rocked back and forth and freed itself from the ground. It fell over toward us and I could see hundreds of fleshy tendrils sticking out of the top of the rock cone. It started running with the finger-like things and dragged itself to the wall. It began pulling itself up the wall with the little tendrils, pulling its rock body behind itself.

I was engrossed in watching this thing climb up the wall, and I had the sudden realization that there could be more of them moving into position above us.

I snapped my head up in time to see a forest of them falling toward us. I had no time to think. I flailed out with my will, connecting to the earth energies and dove on top of Samantha. I willed the stone floor to cover us, as I covered her.

I didn't have time to move a lot of earth from the floor, and I grunted as the stone points from the falling creatures slammed into the thin stone shield and penetrated deep into my rock armor along my back and legs.

Samantha twisted under me. Her face was inches from mine and it was obvious I was in pain. I was pinned to the shield and hung suspended above her. I pictured the ones that missed scrabbling up for another go. I gritted my teeth as the ones stuck in me started to wiggle.

"Should I blink us out?" she asked.

I shook my head. "If we blink into another group of them we will be done for. Hang on," I said.

I closed my eyes and tried to focus past the pain. I attempted to sense all the life energy around us. The ceiling was littered with them, and the ones not busy climbing up the wall were crowding toward us. I felt around for an opening and found a gap in the direction my feet were pointed. In between us and the opening was a huge stone column, thinner in the middle where a stalactite had connected to a stalagmite on the bottom.

"See that big column past my feet?" I asked.

She shifted her body under me and looked where I had indicated, squinting at the darkness. She shook her head and said, "I don't see it, just darkness."

SLAM!

Another one jammed into my shoulder blade and I grunted from the pain. I felt at least four of them piercing my armor now, and the pain was shooting straight to the top of my head.

"It's there," I said through gritted teeth. "We will be safe, if we can get to it."

She nodded, "Here we go!"

She blinked us once, then again. A few more crashed into the ground where we had been. I was no longer suspended over her by the living stalactites, now she held me close as we lay against the column and I healed myself. I wondered if she noticed that I was smelling her hair. It still smelled like apples. I wondered why the girls I like all smelled like fruit. Finally, I was able to stand and pull her up.

She looked me in the eyes and said, "I have lost count of how many times we saved each other in this place."

Then she did something I wasn't ready for. She took my face in her hands and kissed me softly on the cheek. She pulled back from me and I was confused when I saw that her face was very sad.

She turned away from me then and changed the subject, "Why are we safe here?"

I replied, "The creatures travel along the ceiling then release when they are above us. The column is much wider at the top, so they stop at the edge. They are gathered there now on every inch outside of the edge waiting for us to walk away from the column."

I motioned for her to follow me around the column. We hugged it and moved to the other side. I pointed in the direction I had sensed the opening and said, "The exit is that way and there are no more columns to shield us."

I paused then asked, "Samantha, why did you look so sad back there when you kissed my cheek."

She looked at me for a moment then said, "It's nothing."

I replied, frustration in my voice, "Please tell me, I can handle it. Don't treat me like a child."

She motioned for me to sit next to the column and she sat next to me. I realized then that I was weary and sitting felt good. I helped Samantha take the pack off, and I pulled out two apples. We sat against the columns and I waited patiently for her to speak.

She began, picking her words carefully, "It makes me sad to think about what the world will try to do to you, Wess. You are brave and smart, talented and honorable."

"But..." I filled in for what I knew was coming.

Her head dropped a little as she swallowed a bite of apple and she said, "But, they will try to use you for their own purposes or worse, take your life to have what you have rightfully gained. They will see you as a twelve-year-old boy that they can use."

I cleared my throat, "Thirteen."

"Sorry, thirteen. They will all have reasons to use you. Even good people will see something they can gain by knowing you and somehow gaining leverage over you."

"Who is 'they' exactly?" I asked.

She gazed off in the darkness then tossed the apple core into the room.

WHAM!

Almost immediately a rock cone smashed into it. The core exploded from the impact, and the creature started scampering away.

She looked at me then, the sad look back on her face and said, "Everyone, Wess. They will all try."

We sat there for about twenty minutes eating and resting.
I was leaning against the column with my eyes closed,
contemplating what Samantha had said, when I heard
more stalactites slamming into the ground by the door we
came in from. Samantha and I stood up and moved to
investigate. The slamming sound was consistent, and
when we walked around the column we saw why.

The worms had eaten through the door and they were
getting pierced by the hundreds as they slowly crawled
toward us. White goo spattered everywhere as the worms
were impaled by the falling rock creatures. They turned to
eat the stalactites as the stalactites were eating them. It
was pretty much hideous.

"Maybe we should go," I said, "This is nasty."

"Agreed," Samantha said as she slung the pack on.

I reached out with my gift and was pleased to find that all
the ceiling-crawling-rock-cone things had gone to attack
the worms. Once I told Samantha that it was safe, we
walked toward the exit.

When the opening came into view, by the light of the
flaming sword, we started to see another light source past
the opening. We walked toward it and Samantha
sheathed her sword, so we would have better vision in the
dark. Our eyes adjusted and as we got closer we could

make out a man standing on a narrow rock bridge ahead of us.

He was a large, dark-skinned man wearing a sleeveless breastplate. The armor had green runes etched all over it that were glowing. He rested both of his massive wrists on the crossguard of his sword, which was point down on the bridge. The entire blade glowed with a bright white light. In front of the warrior was a yellow line painted on the rock.

We stopped at the opening and studied the area. We were at the beginning of the rock bridge and we could see now that it spanned a large natural cavern. We couldn't see beyond the warrior much as he was effectively blocking the light coming from his sword.

I felt around with my gift and found that there was a river far below us. On the other side, I felt a ledge and could tell that the warrior was right in the middle of the span.

"No, it cannot be. I know this man," Samantha whispered.

I turned to her with my eyebrows raised.

She continued, still staring at him, "I have not seen him since the great wars. His name is Chetan. He was a holy warrior, a force for good everywhere. He wears Emerine, it is one of the seven."

I looked back to the warrior and felt a strong surge of jealousy. Samantha was looking at him with a bit of awe, and I really didn't like it. I was pretty sure she wouldn't call him "cute."

"Well," I said, "let's go say hello to Mr. Muscles."

We walked together and stopped in front of the yellow line. I didn't like the look of it, and felt like Chetan and the line were somehow connected. Chetan stared at us, but otherwise did not move. Now that we were close to him, I was really jealous. He was well over six feet tall with chiseled features and broad shoulders. I was sure any woman would think he was a big stud. Heck, I thought he was a big stud.

"Chetan, do you remember me?" Samantha asked.

Chetan looked at her and furrowed his brow. He looked sad, and then he nodded slowly.

Samantha and I shared a look, then I asked, "Chetan, can you speak?"

Chetan looked at me then slowly shook his head no.

I crossed my arms and stared at him, thinking. "So, this guy has been missing for more than three hundred years?"

"I think so," Samantha said.

I nodded, putting some pieces together. "Chetan, if we cross this yellow line will you attack us?" I asked.

Chetan nodded once.

"Are you under a spell that compels you to do this?"

Nod.

"Did the demon cast the spell?"

Nod.

"Is there a way to break the spell?"

Nod.

I assumed the thinking position, my hand rubbing my chin.

"If we defeat you in battle will we be able to pass then?" Samantha asked.

Chetan shook his head no.

"Hmm, that seemed like the obvious answer," Samantha muttered.

"Exactly," I said, "and the likely path of a great warrior. What if that is exactly what Chetan did? He came here three hundred years ago and defeated whoever was here. When he did, the spell made him assume the role of the guardian. Am I right Chetan?"

Nod.

"And no one has been able to defeat him since," Samantha said, a little too impressed if you asked me.

"So, if we beat him we become the new guardian," I said. "What a beautifully evil spell, it makes sure the strongest guardian holds the bridge."

Samantha spoke, "We must find a way to break the spell without beating him."

"And without entering the spell, I am pretty sure that the first guy to walk in there became the first guardian," I said.

I looked past Chetan, trying to see if there was another line behind him; I couldn't see one. "Wait here," I said, "I want to see where the end of the spell is."

Samantha nodded, and I leapt off the bridge and shifted into an owl. I flew in a wide circle around Chetan until I could see the bridge connecting to a ledge on the far side. On the ground where the bridge ended was another yellow line, matching the one in front.

I turned and flew back to Samantha, landing next to her and dropping the owl form. "As we thought," I said, "there is another yellow line at the back."

"So, the spell is in an area. It stands to reason that if we got him out of it without entering it ourselves; he would be free of the spell."

I nodded and said, "Sounds good, but how do we get him out?"

"We could lasso him and pull." She said.

I countered, "Get into a tug of war with that dude, while we are standing on a rock bridge?"

Both of us shook our heads. I assumed the thinking position once again. If we couldn't move him, maybe I could move the ground he was standing on.

"I have an idea," I said, "Be ready in case he attacks, but don't cross the yellow line."

She nodded and pulled out her flaming sword and dagger. We both backed up from the yellow line, and I focused on the rock beneath Chetan. I considered having the rock buckle and shoot him into the air toward us, but I thought I might break the bridge or send him flying off of it.

Instead, I had the rock shift underneath him and flow slowly toward the yellow line. He moved steadily forward, but as he got close to the line he swiveled his sword upwards in his hands and stepped backward until he was at the original spot. He pivoted the sword point down again and rested his hands.

"He's efficient," I said.

Samantha responded, "I think the spell compels him to stay in it."

I nodded, "Let me try again."

Once again, I started shifting the rock toward us, but this time I was ready. Right before he stepped back I had the rock turn to mud. He sunk into it while I formed the rock up to his knees. At the same time, I sped up the rock sliding on the bridge. Chetan was jerking his legs hard, and as he approached the yellow line he tried to dive backward and landed awkwardly, reaching furiously with his hands.

As soon as he broke the line he stopped struggling. He was lying awkwardly, and I quickly formed the rock over his arms, trapping them above his head. I didn't want to take any chances. This guy looked like he knew how to fight, and I didn't know if he was still under the effects of the spell.

Samantha and I walked up to him, and he turned his head to face us wearing a faraway look and a small smile. He spoke, "You released me from my eternal hell. I will be forever grateful."

As he spoke, I released him from the rock and he laid flat on the bridge. His face began changing as we watched. His cheeks became sunken and his hair turned grey.

Samantha knelt and asked in a concerned voice, "Chetan, what's happening?"

Chetan's voice was a whisper, "I am three hundred and thirty-three years old. I am finally dying. I go to the light. Thank you both."

By the time he was finished speaking, his face had sunken in and his breath was rattling in his chest. Within two more breaths, he was dead. The light of his sword slowly faded, dimming to a dull glow, and as I felt the spark of life leave Chetan completely, the sword turned to a normal dull grey.

Samantha stood back up and before our eyes, Chetan fell to dust.

I looked at Samantha and she had a tear streaming down her cheek. I reached out and took her hand. "Sorry Samantha, I thought we would be gaining a powerful ally. I didn't know we would be killing him," I whispered.

She shook her head, "He was dead the moment he walked into the spell trap, Jerzatu killed him, and I mean to make him pay."

"I think you should take Emerine," I said.

She looked at me with eyes wide, clearly surprised by my comment. "Why would you say that?" She asked.

I shrugged. "I am just a kid. If you take it, we will have a better chance to defeat Jerzatu."

She shook her head. "We could take this back to Sevest right now and be done with this place."

"I hadn't thought of...

My pouch was vibrating. I looked down at it and saw that it was bulging. I reached down to open it, but it ripped and the unicorn statue fell out of it bouncing onto the bridge. It landed upright, and I could see then that it was much larger than when I had found it.

We stepped back as it started humming and growing more rapidly.

"What's happening?" Samantha yelled.

It all clicked for me then, but too late. "Oh no," I said.

I layered myself in rock and put Samantha behind me shuffling backwards.

The unicorn exploded.

A thousand razor sharp shards of jade sliced into me before the blast lifted me off my feet. I landed hard and smashed the back of my skull on the bridge. My ears were ringing and I was seeing double.

I saw two Samanthas, the images moving together then apart. She was hanging on to the side of the bridge barely conscious and sliding slowly over the edge. I saw two Risslings appear on top of the ruined figurine.

I pulled some healing energy into my head and my vision straightened, Rissling became one man. He bent and grabbed the breastplate, a victorious smile on his face. As I stood and pulled my arm back to throw Azurain, the breastplate turned liquid and flowed onto his chest.

Samantha slipped further and I was sure she was about to fall off the bridge. Rissling opened his hand out toward me and a small ball of fire started rolling rapidly along the bridge.

I threw Azurain at him and ran for Samantha.

Rissling twisted his ring while laughing and disappeared.

I snatched Samantha's flaming sword and dove over her, grabbing her pack and yanking her off the bridge by the straps as the fireball exploded behind me.

I felt no heat as we were engulfed in flame; Samantha's sword protected me. My body mostly shielded Samantha's, but as we sailed out from the bridge I flowed regenerative energy into her. I felt her wounds from the jade shards and the blast healing even as we tumbled through the air. I tried to remain calm as we spun and twisted, but it didn't help when Samantha woke and clutched me in panic.

I tuned it all out and closed my eyes, feeling all the rock around me and the water in the river below that we were now rushing toward. I knew that I could change into an owl or eagle and be fine, but there was no way I was leaving Samantha to fall to her death.

I pulled her close to me and she wrapped me in a fear driven hug with her legs and arms. I felt her trembling as we plummeted. I focused on the water and tried to decide what I wanted it to do. I knew that if I had it rush upwards to meet us we would just die higher. I needed a way to slow our fall without the impact.

I called the water from way up the river. I called the entire river. It was more water than I had ever moved, but desperation and focus drove my need. I pulled the river into the air and had it flow above us in an arc so that when we entered it we would be falling at the same rate as the water. This all happened within seconds, but it felt like forever.

It was a strange sensation to enter the water at full falling speed, but have it feel like I was slipping into a still stream. I put a bubble of air over the two of us and then slowed the water gradually until we were at ground level. I had the river place us gently on the ground and I helped Samantha to stand and handed her sword back.

"I don't want to ever do that again," she said, her voice shaking a little. She took a deep breath and shook her arms out to try and get control.

I looked back at the river still flowing in the massive arc and smiled, saying, "I actually thought it was awesome. I think I could sell tickets to that. Plus, I got the biggest hug from you ever, so I think this was pretty much a win for me."

I let the river go back to its natural state and released the massive flow of energy I had been holding. Exhaustion rolled over me like a wave from the ocean. I felt like I would fall where I stood. Suddenly, I was cold, tired and hungry all at once.

I walked to the cavern wall and slumped against it, sliding to a sitting position. Samantha sat next to me and laid the sword by our feet. Now that I wasn't holding it, I felt its heat and I began drying my wet boots on it.

"Couldn't you just ask the water to leave your boots or something?" Samantha asked.

I stared at my boots and then looked at her. "Duh," I said.

With a tiny trickle of energy I had the water group up then squirt out of my toes back into the river. I did the same for Samantha and we were both instantly dry. "Your boots are making pee-pee," I said.

She giggled and pulled a blanket and pillow from the pack and handed them over.

"I am a moron," I said as I took them. "I shouldn't have taken that stupid unicorn for Myka. Rissling played me for a fool. I mean, how obvious is that? There are five empty alcoves but hey, here is a pretty unicorn just for the moron kid!"

I lay on the blanket and Samantha started softly petting my head. She whispered, "Go to sleep, I will watch for trouble."

I had more to say, we had plans to make. We needed to decide if we should go back up to the bridge or try and find a path down here. I was having the conversation in my head, my brain too muddled to realize that I wasn't actually talking. I was so tired that it was like someone turned a switch off. There was no drifting this time, I was just suddenly asleep.

I started dreaming almost immediately. I dream a lot when I sleep and sometimes I can actually control what is happening. In those dreams, I always beat the bad guys and get the girl. I do this without powers; in those dreams I am just so manly that I can beat everyone up. I like those dreams, but this wasn't one of those.

In this dream, I was observing a scene playing out as I floated above it. In most dreams, the details are lost to me. My brain focuses on me whopping the bad guys, not the color of the floor or the smells. Details like that are left to my waking hours, but again in this regard this dream was different.

I was in a large room with six pillars made of granite. I floated above and behind a sorcerer holding a book in his left hand, his other hand moving in complex patterns. The sorcerer's entire left arm was clad in a glowing orange beautifully etched plate armor sleeve. Seven braziers burned a foul smelling substance and the black greasy smoke danced in a circular pattern over symbols etched on the ground.

Inside the pattern stood a creature twice the height of the spell-caster. It had yellow eyes and mottled green and black scales with folded bat wings. Its head had a large fanged snout and it had large goat like horns twisting off of it. At the end of its right arm was a huge pincer like claw. I could feel its hate pouring from it as it stared at the sorcerer with fiery eyes.

I knew I was witnessing the scene from six hundred years ago when Alawaice bound the demon to protect this place. This was no dream; it was a vision of the past that for some reason I was able to watch now.

Alawaice finished casting and spoke, "I bind you Jerzatu! I bind you to a contract for one thousand years!"

Jerzatu responded, his fangs flashing as he spoke, "You over reach human! Even with that artifact your soul will be mine if you should die before the contract ends! No human lives forever and you are already old! Name your terms human, I shall enjoy rending your soul for eternity when you die an old man!"

Alawaice spoke calmly, "You will guard me and my treasures, creating all manner of devious traps to kill any that would attempt to reach me here to the best of your ability."

"You desire solitude human? So much so that you are willing to give up your soul? You will be dead within forty years at the most. I accept your terms, with the joy of knowing that your soul will be my new plaything soon enough!" Jerzatu sneered.

"I bind you Jerzatu, for the term of one thousand years or until I die." Alawaice mumbled something I couldn't hear and moved his hand in intricate patterns in the air. As he did, a series of black runes formed one by one in a circle around the demon. When the circle was complete the smoke glowed orange then dissipated.

Jerzatu stepped from the circle and shouted, "What a fool you are Alawaice. Forty years is nothing for a demon!"

Alawaice pulled the largest diamond from his pocket that I have ever seen and held it up. "The irony of this amuses me demon. You promised to protect all my treasures and this gem contains my greatest treasure, my soul! I will never die as long as it is safe. In another thousand years I will bind you again! By then, I will be even more powerful than I am today, my mastery over the arcane arts will allow me to do anything with this much time!"

The demon roared his anger and I woke in the cavern, confused about where I was. I sat up and looked around, Samantha stood on the other side of her sword watching me with a concerned look on her face.

"How long was I asleep?" I asked with a groggy voice.

Samantha crouched next to me and pushed my hair back examining my forehead. She answered me finally, "About twelve hours. I was unable to wake you."

She looked at my eyes then, apparently satisfied with my forehead, and I asked, "Is there something on my head?"

She smiled and said, "Not on it, but in it." She helped me stand, and my legs were a little shaky. "Shortly after you went to sleep a blue orb came out from that wall and entered your forehead. It happened so quickly that I couldn't even react. I tried everything to wake you, including dumping water on you."

"I think the demon sent me a vision," I said while studying the wall.

"Really?" Samantha asked, "What did you see?"

I relayed dream, "It was from when Alawaice bound Jerzatu to his contract. Jerzatu assumed he would die soon and he would get the sorcerers soul, but Alawaice put his soul in a diamond so he wouldn't."

"So, that means Alawaice is still alive?" She asked.

I thought for a moment then shared my theory, "Well, I think the demon must have set that dream orb to record the scene prior to being bound. He is now bound to protect Alawaice and his treasures until one thousand years or until Alawaice dies. Jerzatu gets Alawaice's soul if he dies so he must still be alive, at least in some form."

"If we kill Alawaice, the demon will be released. So, we may not need to fight him?" She asked.

"Or we will need to fight them both. I think we must be prepared for the two of them," I said.

Samantha asked, "Where are they?"

I closed my eyes and reached out with my gift. I felt through the stone where Samantha had said the blue orb had come from. I knew what the room looked like now where Alawaice had performed his ritual. I sent tiny probes out in all directions and quickly came to a large open space forward and down, not far from where we were standing. The stone lining the room was granite cut in long flat pieces. They were supported by six massive stone columns. There were two openings to the room off to the left and right.

I opened my eyes and said, "I believe they are below us right there." I pointed down to the joint where the wall met the ground. "I could open a tunnel. We stand no more than six feet from the room where Alawaice summoned Jerzatu more than six hundred years ago."

Samantha shook her head, "We need a plan," She said, "Did you see where he put the soul gem?"

"No," I said, "it ended before I could see that."

"Can you sense it? Like you did with the emerald?" She asked.

I responded, "I hadn't thought to do that. Let me try." I reached out with my gift again and searched inside the room with the six pillars. In the back of the room, I sensed a large diamond about waist high. "It's in there, at the back of the room," I said.

Samantha nodded. "The only thing that matters is destroying that gem. So, you open the tunnel and I will blink us to the back of the room. We strike fast and hit it with Azurain," she proposed.

I countered, "It could be trapped. I can break a diamond with my earth flows from across the room. I think we should not approach it unless my powers fail for some reason. If it isn't working I will throw Azurain and if that doesn't work, only then do we blink to it."

She nodded, "If either of them is there then I will distract them, you must focus on the diamond."

I nodded. "It's a plan, ready?" I asked.

She moved to my right and put her left hand on my shoulder, holding her flame blade out in front of her. She looked at me and took a deep breath, then dipped her chin.

"One last thing," I said, "If I should fall, you should teleport to safety."

She looked at me with hardness in her blue eyes and said, "No."

I knew it was pointless to argue, I felt the same way about my new friend. We had only been together for two days now, but we had been through so much together I wouldn't leave her either, for any reason. I smiled at her, knowing it was pointless to argue. I took a deep breath and used my will to carve a tunnel to the room below.

Chapter 22: Soul Gem

The room opened below us. I barely had time to register that it was well lit with braziers before Samantha blinked us inside. As my gift had shown me, the room held six pillars and two open halls, one to my left and one right. Both of them curved toward the back of the room so I couldn't see far down them.

On the floor in front of me was the familiar pattern from my dream and behind that was a wooden pillar with the huge diamond on a stand.

There was no one in the room with us, and I whispered, "This is too easy. Why would he display the one thing that can kill him?"

Samantha whispered in response, "He probably wasn't thinking that someone would leap off the bridge then tunnel in through the roof. Just break it; we won't trigger any traps from here."

I still wasn't sure, it didn't feel right, but I didn't like the idea of going and looking for Alawaice and maybe running into Jerzatu instead. I decided Samantha was probably right.

I reached out with my gift and was surprised to find a large fissure in the center of the gem stone. I made a very subtle wedge with an earth flow and pried at the flaw.

The stone cracked right down the center and fell off the stand.

A deep bell rang one single bong before the pieces hit the ground and the smoke from the braziers began to swirl together.

"This isn't good," Samantha said, "I think you were right."

The flames in the braziers shot up and then leaned into the middle of the rune circle. The flames bent together and a creature took shape in the midst of all the fire. The flames painted themselves to the bottom of the creature revealing a massive red skinned beast with black straight horns. Had we been standing at the diamond it would have cooked us alive as it manifested.

It opened its eyes, smiled, and then shot its arms out. Flames flew from its hands in a wide column toward each of us. I dove behind the stone pillar and the heat poured into it. I summoned wind and forced it to keep the flames from wrapping around it.

Samantha took a different tactic; she blinked right to the creature, stood in the flames, and started hacking on it. The creature howled in fury and turned both of its flame columns on her. They weren't hurting her at all, but Samantha's sword didn't seem to be doing anything to the creature either.

I yelled to her, "The braziers Samantha! They are feeding it!"

Samantha spun and kicked out with her heel, spilling the brazier and the burning coals out on the floor. The flames continued to feed the creature, and I knew I had to be more creative.

Apparently, the creature realized that Samantha was immune to fire because it decided to punch her instead. Samantha was blinking all around it as it flailed at her in all directions. Samantha was striking it easily enough and had kicked over three more fire pots, but it wasn't getting us anywhere.

I closed my eyes and reached out with my gift toward the river. I grabbed the water and formed it into a ball. I pulled it down the tunnel I had opened and flung it toward the fire creature. The ball was as large as the rune circle and I made sure it that it hit all the coals.

Steam rose from the creature and the coals as the water ball struck them. The creature wailed in pain and its skin turned a dull black. Samantha blinked right behind it and jammed her sword through its back. I stepped out to throw Azurain, but I caught a glimpse of movement from the corner of my right eye.

I turned in time to see Jerzatu reach out and grab me around the waist with a huge pincer hand. My rock armor saved me, and I lifted Azurain to strike him as he lifted me off the ground.

I heard a boom from the other hall. I flailed out with my gift as I turned in time to see a lightning bolt flying at me. I grabbed the bolt with my mind and barely deflected it into Jerzatu's face. Even though it didn't hit me, the shock carried through his arm and made my jaw clench it was so powerful.

Jerzatu dropped on his back and flopped around. His claw opened and I rolled out, standing quickly.

Stepping into the light was Alawaice, or what used to be Alawaice. He was a skeletal creature now with red glowing eyes. I only knew it was him because he wore orange glowing armor on his left arm.

He was casting another spell, his arms gesturing toward me. Samantha appeared next to him and jammed her sword into his side. It disrupted his casting, but his left arm shot out and grabbed her around the throat. His rictus smile never changing. I guess it was tough for him to change his expression since his lips had rotted off.

This goofy thought went through my head as I stepped forward and threw Azurain with all my strength. Even as it was tumbling through the air, Samantha was being covered in frost radiating outward from Alawaice's hand. Her eyes were wide, and I could tell she was in pain. I started to flow healing energy into her as I ran toward her, following my spinning weapon. My axe struck Alawaice in his armored arm and it spun him in a circle from the force, discarding Samantha in the process. She went to one knee grabbing at her frozen throat.

Azurain appeared back in my hand I and I threw again, all the while healing Samantha. My axe spun true and as the sorcerer stopped spinning from my first hit it buried itself deep in its skull.

Alawaice flopped backward and Samantha grabbed her sword from his side. "Look out!" She screamed and disappeared. I dove and rolled as Jerzatu's claw snapped shut where my neck had been a moment ago.

I rolled to a stand and made Azurain appear back in my hand. Samantha had engaged the demon and they were both moving so fast that I was having trouble watching them.

"Find the Gem!" she yelled.

I turned and ran toward Alawaice with the intent of running past him and searching the other room. Unfortunately, the undead sorcerer was rising like he had hinges in his freaking heels.

The gaping wound in his head was starting to close, but I could still see his brains. This dude was seriously gross, but I guess he looked pretty good for a six hundred-year-old.

I swung Azurain at his neck, but he raised Ambress and deflected it. Orange runes flared on his armguard and blue flared on my axe. He flung his right hand toward me and I sensed water energy pulling into his hand. I was prepared when he shot a cone of frost toward me; I bent it back on him with my will. It coated him in frost and slowed him enough that I was able to jam Azurain up into his ribs.

I left it there and sprinted past him moving to the right of the hallway so he would lose visibility quicker as the hallway was also bending to the right. I made the turn and summoned Azurain back to my hand as I burst into a new room.

It was a combination lab and library and was well lit from a bright white globe above me. There were no visible exits from the room, so I stepped inside to the right to remove myself from visibility of the hall.

I closed my eyes and reached out with my gift quickly scanning for any diamonds. I felt lots of copper and even some gold in the lab equipment, but no diamond.

I opened my eyes in time to see three black tentacles reaching around the corner toward me. I jumped backward and swiped with my magical axe, severing the closest one. The second one shot out at me, wrapped around my legs, and yanked. As I fell backwards, I swiped the third one and chopped it in half.

The one around my legs yanked me rapidly into the hall. It was pulling me into a gaping black hole that had opened in the middle of the floor. To make matters worse, Alawaice was standing in the hall, and as I watched, he shot both hands out at me, completing another spell. Four green arrows shot from his hands and flew in my direction while I was dragged toward the hole.

I reacted quickly, and looking back I can say without a doubt that my brain before I had Azurain could not have come up with a solution to both my problems in such a short time.

I reached out with my will and urged the rock to move quickly. Stone shot up from the floor in reaction to my need and smashed the tentacle into the ceiling. This had the extra benefit of blocking the four arrows. I was lifted off the ground a little before the tentacle went limp. As the tentacle was dropping me, I heard explosions rocking the wall on the other side.

I ran back into the lab I had just left and created a tunnel into the room with Jerzatu and Samantha. I ran through and was overjoyed to see blink girl still holding her own against the demon. Unfortunately, the demon was healing everything she was doing to it. She was way too fast for it, but I knew that eventually she would tire. One hit would probably be the end of my friend.

I thought I might help a little or at least give Samantha a well needed break. As I ran past, I hurled Azurain into Jerzatu's back. It buried itself deep into the creature's spine and he stumbled, reaching for my weapon. He shouldn't have bothered since Azurain reappeared in my hand as I ran down the hall. I hoped that Alawaice didn't know I had left the hallway and was still working on getting through my makeshift wall. I didn't like the idea of Samantha fighting both of them at once.

This hall curved quickly to my left and I came upon another room in the same location as the one on the other side. The only difference was that this room held a large stone staircase going up; I assumed back toward the bridge. Racks of shelves holding jars of materials filled the room and I imagined that this was where Alawaice kept the components for his spells. Once again, I reached out with my power and searched for a diamond.

There was nothing in the room and my heart sank. I sent my gift up the staircase and felt that it continued on for a great while, but there was no trace of a diamond anywhere.

I ran back to the main room, ready to tell Samantha that it was time to flee, that our plan had failed. As I rounded the corner, I was blown backward as a massive fireball exploded in the room. I smashed into the curved wall and slid down it. The heat was unbearable, and I was sure that I was going to have to re-grow some eyebrows.

Just as soon as it had filled the room the fire snuffed out. Samantha, Alawaice and Jerzatu all stood in the room, completely unharmed by the fire.

Alawaice began casting again and I stood. Suddenly, I was hit with a realization. I had to think like a sorcerer who wanted to guard his soul so much that he was willing to summon an indestructible demon to protect it. Where would I put that gem?

I knew the answer before I even reached out with my gift. I flailed out urgently with my probe as Alawaice finished his casting. Nine blue missiles traced random paths toward Samantha, as she fought the demon. Alawaice stood there pointing at her with his bony finger.

My probe hit Jerzatu and I felt the diamond immediately. It was in his right chest muscle, just below the skin. I had no time for subtlety, so I lashed at the stone with my gift. The gem didn't crack like the last one did, it exploded violently.

The demon's chest erupted and Samantha was showered in gore and shards. The demon roared in triumph, *"YES!"*

Alawaice exploded as well and the blue missiles each popped into thin air just before striking Samantha. Ambress fell to the ground with a noisy clang.

Jerzatu turned to me slowly, and Samantha blinked to me, her sword held out in front of her. I couldn't help but notice that her hair was plastered to her face and she was covered with sweat. She wasn't breathing as hard as I would have been though, so I had to give her some credit.

Jerzatu roared, "I am free and the sorcerer's soul is mine! His torment shall be legendary!"

Jerzatu was fading, I could see through his wings now. He looked at me then and studied me intently. "I shall remember you boy, and I vow to go easy on you should you ever find yourself in my realm!" he said.

Then he simply disappeared. I turned to Samantha and said, "So, I've got that going for me!"

She fell into me then, her forehead resting on my shoulder as she giggled. Finally, she pulled back and said, "I am glad I didn't kill you when I met you, Wess."

I hugged her for real and responded, "I'm glad you got a chance to work with me too."

We walked over to Ambress and Samantha handed me the pack. "I am going to destroy his spell books," she said.

"I didn't take you for a book burner Samantha," I quipped.

As she walked past Alawaice's remains she called back to me, "The world can do just fine without this knowledge!"

I crouched down and called the blanket from the pack. I took it and wrapped the armor in the blanket twice. I tied it tight, so I wouldn't accidentally touch it when I went to pull it from the pack. I slid Ambress in and stood as Samantha was returning.

"I found something," she said.

She held a cube in her hand. It was smooth metal with no seams. It was about the size of my open palm.

"What is it?" I asked.

She shrugged, "I have no idea, but it appears solid and is light as a feather. It is like no metal I have seen before."

I opened the side pocket that we had kept the light tube in before I lost it and held it open for her. She dropped it in and said, "Maybe Sevest will know what it is."

A bell went off in my head, "Samantha, right before the unicorn exploded, you mentioned Sevest's name."

"I did?" she shrugged, "What of it?

I responded, "Rissling appeared at just the right time. It makes me think he was watching or listening to us somehow. If he heard you say the name Sevest, he would know that we are working with him. If he connects us to Sevest he will likely know that Sevest is the one who rescued my mom, assuming Sevest has been successful while we were down here."

Samantha stared at me for a moment, "Then we have no time to waste!"

She grabbed my shoulder and rolled her ring on the hilt of her sword.

We blinked into a hellish scene. The entire left half of Sevest's home was a smoking ruin. The front door stood ajar, bashed off its hinges. Sevest's snake guards lay burned and twisted at odd angles. Huge blast marks in between them.

We spun when we heard Rissling's voice, louder than it should have been, booming out above and behind us, "Warriors, the courtyard is clear! Bring me Sevest and the mother. Slaughter the rest."

Rissling floated above us in the air, shouting at a horde of Lord Algrier's dragon warriors. He was pointing behind him at Sevest's house. He wore Emerine, the green rune covered breastplate that Chetan had on. Apparently, he had not seen us as he was facing away from the building, shouting at the army of warriors. I thought about throwing Azurain at him, but as the dragon humanoids charged, Samantha grabbed me and blinked again.

We appeared right inside the door of the estate, where four of the snake guards stood waiting with spears leveled at us.

"Where is Sevest?" I asked urgently.

The snakes just stared at us, their tongues darting out and wiggling. They showed no sign that they recognized us or weren't about to impale us.

"They're coming. Can you slow them down, Wess?" Samantha asked.

I turned back to the opening and saw hundreds of the armored dragon knights charging us at full run. I pulled energy in and focused my will on the stairs. I made the stone flow up from them and cover the doorway. I kept it flowing until the stairs were gone and the doorway was blocked with four feet of solid stone.

"Your timing is impeccable," Sevest whispered in my ear.

Samantha and I both jumped. "Dude! I wish you could just walk in a freaking room like a normal person!"

Sevest spread his hands and said, "Alas, I am not a normal person."

There was a crash on the wall from outside, and the entire room shook.

Sevest gazed at the wall and said, "I suppose we should get your mother and Mr. Millen and be on our way; the house will not stand long."

He turned and walked quickly past the guards into the hallway. The snakes fell into line behind us without a word from Sevest, and it made me wonder how they communicated. We went down a staircase and Sevest asked over his shoulder, "So, I am assuming you have something for me, Wess?"

Samantha passed me the pack and I pulled the bundle out and passed it up to Sevest. There was another huge crash from above and it sounded like the ceiling had collapsed.

Sevest un-wrapped Ambress and discarded the blanket. As soon as he grabbed the artifact it flowed up his left arm and glowed a soft orange. I glimpsed a purple glow out of the top of his right boot that flared up at the same time. Sevest continued walking, but handed a ring back to Samantha and said, "My dear, would you please trade me rings? This one will take us to Swansea and I would like yours so that I may return when I am ready to deal with Rissling."

Samantha took the ring off her thumb and passed it to Sevest. She put the new one in its place. Sevest reached a door and quickly went inside. I followed Sevest inside and froze at the door.

My mother rose slowly from the couch at the far side. She was thinner than I remembered, but looked perfect to me.

"Wesslayn!" she called as she rushed toward me. Tears burst from her eyes and mine responded in kind. I charged past Sevest and wrapped her in a hug that would have made Hannah Bear proud.

She was sobbing on my shoulder, and I was suddenly embarrassed to see Mr. Millen standing behind her. I had only ever seen Mr. Millen serious, working, and kind of scary. Now he was covering his mouth and tears were trickling down his face.

Samantha spoke behind us, "They're coming, folks! Let's have this reunion in Swansea!"

I pulled away from my mother and realized the sounds of battle were coming from the hall behind us.

"I need everyone to be touching me," Samantha said as she walked to us.

Sevest said, "Well if you insist my dear. So forward, though. I am used to being the one to court beautiful women." He stood close to Samantha and put his hand around her waist.

I smiled when I noticed Samantha was blushing and Sevest was purring. I took Samantha's hand and gestured for Mr. Millen to come over. He seemed unsure about what was happening, so I said, "We are leaving, Mr. Millen. Quickly, please touch Samantha so we can take you to Myka."

His eye went wide as he processed what I was saying. He stepped close, and my mother and he placed their hands on Samantha's forearm.

"What about your guards?" I asked.

Sevest shrugged and said, "They are doing what they are supposed to."

There was an explosion in the hall and flames rolled toward us. Samantha activated the ring as I was shielding my face from the heat.

We blinked, the temporary darkness quickly replaced by the Swansea throne room. I laughed when I realized that Sevest had set the ring inside the throne room. He could have set it anywhere. He was showing off, I think.

We all stepped away from Samantha when we arrived, except for Sevest. He was rubbing his cheek on her shoulder over and over.

"Umm, what are you doing?" she asked as guards moved toward us from the door.

"Just putting my scent on you, my sweet thing, I wouldn't want another kitty to claim you," Sevest purred.

I couldn't help but laugh when Samantha grabbed his snout and shoved him off of her.

The guards arrived then, and I looked around for a face I recognized. I had seen them before, but I couldn't remember any names. When they saw me they raised their halberds and looked more relaxed, but they were still looking at Sevest with great interest.

"Gentlemen, could you let my father and Myka know we are back?" I asked.

The guard closest to me snapped his heals together and said, "Right away, Wess!"

"Oh, and you may want to let the king know too, we should probably update him on the situation in Kurzak." I added.

My mom started babbling about how much I had grown and asking about when the last time I had my hair cut was. She asked something about me keeping up with my reading, but I was busy eavesdropping on Samantha and Sevest.

Samantha pulled the metal cube out and was asking Sevest if he knew what it was.

"Oh indeed I do," he said, "That is an instant fortress. They are very rare and powerful. One simply throws it on the ground and an indestructible tower will spring up. However, it only works outside; a wise safeguard from its creator, no doubt."

Samantha smiled at Sevest, and I have to admit I felt pangs of jealousy.

"Wess?" my mom asked.

"Oh sorry Mom, yes I kind of had a bath last night when I had a river change its flow to keep Samantha and me from splatting into the ground."

"Wesslayn there is no reason to be smart with me. Your friend Sevest has informed me about all your new *powers* and your *special* axe, but I am still your mom," she said with her hands on her hips.

I couldn't help it, I started to giggle and I hugged her, "I missed you, Mom. I will take a bath tonight and let you cut my hair, I promise."

"Wess!" A girlish shriek exploded behind me and I spun, hopping to see Myka. Instead, Princess Erin crashed into me, actually leaping into a hug and threatening to knock me over. I laughed as she cranked down tight on my neck.

Then suddenly she released me and said, "Oh, a cat person!" She slid off me and walked to Sevest.

My mom pushed me forward and whispered, "Introduce the princess!"

I quickly went to Princess Erin's side and said, "Princess Erin I would like to introduce you to my new friends. This is Sevest, he is from Kurzak."

Sevest performed a perfect bow and Princess Erin executed a curtsy while giggling.

"And this is Samantha, Queen of the Elves," I added.

Samantha stepped forward and nodded her head as an equal would. She smiled and said, "Pleased to meet you Your Highness."

I was about to introduce Mr. Millen and my Mother, but from the doorway I heard Myka's voice, "Daddy!"

She ran across the room and embraced her father. I looked over at my mother, but she was walking away from me with her arms out and tears in her eyes. My father came to her and they embraced. He picked her up and twirled her in a hug. "I didn't think I would ever see you again," she said.

I stood there feeling awkward as Princess Erin furiously questioned Sevest and Samantha the way only a nine-year-old could, "Do you have claws? Do you eat mice? Can I see your fangs? How old are you? I thought all elves were dead. How many are there? Do you all have pointy ears? Is it true that you can see in the dark? Do you have a castle?"

Myka hadn't even looked at me, she was so busy with her father. My mom and dad were pretty focused on each other. I started fidgeting, not sure what to do, when I heard familiar stomps that could only belong to someone made of four hundred pounds of muscle. I turned in time to see Ben stoop to clear the doorway.

I heard Samantha draw her sword behind me and I quickly said, "No, he is with us. He is my friend Ben."

"Oh, you have a flaming sword," Erin said. "Can I hold it? Don't worry, Ben gives great piggy-back rides!"

Ben ignored everything and came straight to me and patted me awkwardly on the head. "Hi," he said.

"Hi Ben, glad to see you. I am sorry I couldn't take you with me on this trip, we really could have used you a few times," I said.

Ben was still patting my head. It cracked me up that someone could be so fluid in battle and so completely awkward in a situation like this.

"Yes, so about the whole leaving without saying goodbye thing, Wess," my dad said.

"Yes," Myka said. "Please tell us what happened. I am dying to know what could have prevented you from even saying goodbye three days ago."

I looked from my father's stern expression to Myka's icy glare. "This really isn't going how thought it would. I was hoping for something more like hey, Wess, thanks for saving our family members!" I said.

I was about to say more when the guards by the door slammed their halberds into the ground, and the king entered. He was wearing informal clothes and didn't have his normal team of people that ran around behind him everywhere.

We all turned and knelt except for Samantha, Sevest and Erin. Erin was whispering to Sevest, "That's my dad, he's the king."

"Please stand, my friends." The king said as walked to us.

The king went straight to my mother and said, "Rebecca, it is wonderful to see you again, it has been too long since your beauty graced my halls." He kissed her on the cheek.

She blushed and curtsied, "You are too kind, Your Grace."

"Huh, that's where I get it from," I muttered, observing the rosy bloom on her cheeks.

The king turned to me and said, "Wess, I suspect you have some stories to tell us and maybe a hole to dig your way out of, but first, why don't you introduce me to your friends?"

"Yes, Your Grace, this is Sevest from Kurzak and Samantha, Queen of the Elves."

The king looked at me with a strange look, "Wess, you never fail to surprise me. What marvelous guests you have brought us."

He went to Samantha first and said, "My lady, it is good to have you in my hall. I never met your mother, but the stories I have heard about her have shown her to be a wise woman who did whatever was necessary to care for her people. I hope that one day we can be allies again as our kingdoms were in centuries past."

Samantha responded, "Your Highness, I believe the time for that discussion is upon us, my people have returned to this realm and are in need of a home to call their own."

King William smiled and looked genuinely happy about the news. He said, "Elves in Faermont again, I had thought this was a bridge too far. I look forward to talking with you on this, and I am confident we can come to an agreement."

The king stepped over to Sevest next and offered his hand. Sevest shook it and said, "I am honored, Your Majesty."

The king asked, "Sevest, are you a representative of a particular noble?"

Sevest shook his head, "Not anymore, but on this subject I believe we have much to discuss, Your Highness. We have a shared enemy in Rissling. Unfortunately, he has gained Emerine and now knows that I have worked against him."

The chief steward came huffing in and stood quietly by the door. The king addressed the room, "I would like to propose that we meet for dinner this evening and discuss all that has happened. We will make a plan for the elves and for Kurzak."

The king turned to me then and said, "Well, my life has been filled with interesting new changes since you came into it, Wess. I think we should also celebrate your birthday this evening. I understand we missed one while you were having your adventure?"

He said it like I was playing a childhood game like knights and nobles. I responded awkwardly, "Oh, yes, Your Grace, but really, there is no need. Dinner would be wonderful though."

"Until tonight then!" he said. Then he turned and walked out, summoning the steward to relay his plan. I was pretty sure I heard him say, "cakes."

The younger, good looking steward came in and offered to take Sevest and Samantha to their guest rooms. My mom made a motion toward Myka, who was still purposefully not looking at me. Samantha and Sevest left the room with Erin trailing them, all the while peppering them with questions.

I walked over to Myka and waited patiently to talk to her. I knew she saw me, but she ignored me completely and said, "Maybe we should head to the room and clean up, Daddy."

I was trying to think of what to say, but Mr. Millen saved me. He said, "Wess, Sevest told me that you got me added into the agreement and I just wanted to say thank you. I was working as a baker for one of the other lords and Sevest purchased me from him. Turns out, I make a pretty good cake, so I think he paid a pretty penny for me. Anyway, I just wanted to say thank you. You will always have a place in front of my hearth if you want it and I am so glad you got your parents back."

He turned to Myka and just stared at her; finally she sighed and turned to me. She spoke in an unemotional tone, "Thank you for rescuing my father, Wess."

Her anger caught me by surprise. I didn't know what to say, so of course, I said the wrong thing, "Umm, no problem."

Now her fangs really came out, "I guess it wasn't a problem since you got to run around with your new girlfriend. She is very pretty. I can see why you didn't want to waste your time saying goodbye to someone like me."

I tried to respond, I think I was stammering stuff about a unicorn figurine that exploded in my face as she stomped out. Mr. Millen and I shared a look and he said, "I would love to give you advice on women, Wess, but I never learned how to talk to any of them. When Myka's mom would get mad at me, I would bake something for her." He shrugged and said, "Thanks again, see you tonight."

I didn't know how to cook anything so I was pretty sure I was doomed. I turned to my parents, who were sharing a smile; I'm sure at my expense.

My dad looked at me and said, "This hero thing is pretty hard, huh?"

My shoulders slumped and I said, "I am just not sure I'm cut out for any of it."

My mom pulled me into a group hug and my dad said, "I think you are doing pretty well, Wess. I don't think you are going to have much of a choice, though. It seems that you are destined for big things, like it or not."

Epilogue

That night we had a dinner and a private party celebrating my thirteenth birthday. Everyone was well-dressed and cleaned up and I have to say that it was hard not to stare at Samantha in a dress. She was simply stunning. The king insisted that Samantha and I tell the entire story from our adventure. It turned out that Samantha wasn't a very good story teller. She would summarize an epic battle with, "and then we killed them all."

I ended up telling most of it, and Myka glared at me up until I got to the unicorn part. She wouldn't look at me after that, she just moved her food around on her plate.

My mom looked horrified through most of it, and I thought my dad was going to burst from pride. He slapped the table when I relayed the ogre fights. He said he wished he could have been there to see it.

When I got to the math puzzles I posed them to the group for fun. Myka thought about it then said, "Obviously, I am not as smart as Samantha!"

Sevest waited patiently for everyone to guess for a while and then shared the solution, confident in his answers. I noticed he asked a lot of detailed questions about the traps. They seemed to fascinate him.

When I got to the part about the unicorn exploding and being a trap, Sevest nodded and said, "Well it all makes sense now."

He said that he had framed another lord for stealing my mom and that Rissling had even started forays against the other house in response. Rissling had suddenly stopped and attacked his house without warning. He had no idea how Rissling had figured it out until now.

He called it a tether spell and said that they are quite common in Kurzak and that you could even purchase scrolls so that non-wizards could cast them. The spell allowed Rissling to watch and hear us through a crystal scrying orb. Sevest seemed to know a lot about the subject.

When I talked about ending slavery in Kurzak, my mom's face went pale. Mr. Millen shared a few stories about what he had seen while he was there. He talked about how slaves were routinely tortured or killed.

He got a tear in his eye when he described a kitchen maid that was no older than Myka. He had grown quite fond of her and named her mouse because she always scurried under foot. He said she spilled an expensive pitcher of wine one day and she just disappeared after that.

He looked at me then and said that I was doing the right thing and that if he had powers or could wield a sword he would be right there with me. He said that the Lords of Kurzak were pure evil.

After all the stories, the king vowed to support the elves in any way he could. He offered to build a road to their new home in the forest and to officially recognize it as their sovereign lands. Samantha bristled at that a little, saying that all of this land was theirs long before it was ours. She quickly backed off and apologized then thanked the king for his generosity.

She said she would consider the offer of the road, but would need to talk with her people. They needed to decide if they wanted to be active in the realms or stay hidden. She said it would not be a decision she would force on her people.

The king said he needed to discuss the situation in Kurzak with his advisors in the morning and invited Sevest, Samantha, and I to share our plan with them as well. Sevest thanked the king and I wondered what plan we would share, since as far as I knew we didn't really have one.

A cake was brought out then and Mr. Millen announced that he had baked it for my birthday. As we ate it Sevest pulled Samantha and I aside and said, "I just wanted to remind you of your vow to help me free my country from slavery. I am going back to do just that and I will be expecting your assistance."

I looked over at my parents, then Myka, who was presently eyeballing Samantha's dress. "Yeah," I said, "I will keep my word."

Samantha nodded, "We will cut off the heads of the snakes and lead a revolution in Kurzak."

I turned back to them and said, "We have to finish it in seven days though, it is all I have left before I have to go to training."

Samantha smiled and said, "Look what we did in the last three…"

I watched Myka refuse her cake and leave the room, "Yeah," I said, "real heroic stuff."

I was afraid to tell Myka I would be leaving again in the morning.

Made in the USA
Lexington, KY
06 August 2013